T.O.R.N.

THERE'S ONLY RIGHT NOW

Ampora Yazdani

Acknowledgements

I would like to acknowledge the works of Eckhart Tolle and Neville Goddard for their inspiring words on presence which has heavily influenced my heart, mind, and imagination.

Dedication

To my mother, father, and brother thank you for all of your love and encouragement whispered through the cosmos into the seat of my soul.

To my husband, Farhad, and children Obadias, Farrah, and Soraya you have given me an opportunity to know love in ways I never dreamt possible, this story is dedicated to you.

Chapter 1
Stella

Inhale. The sound of flowing water from the electric fountain tickled the hair on the back of Stella's neck.

Exhale. Tension from her spine released through her breath.

Stretch. Her muscles pulled the stress from the day before out of her body through the tips of her fingers.

Inhale. The soft Zen music playing from her bedroom stereo bounced off the tranquil pallet of muted corals that enriched the walls and enveloped her.

Let go. All of it disappeared into an expanse of weightlessness that blanketed her soul as she closed her eyes and opened her sight to peace. But in the calm, something was amiss.

Serene, Stella's morning ritual had become her constant in a reality that challenged her to the marrow of her bones. Her meditations and gentle affirmations brought her back from the despondent edge of a sea of melancholy to the peaks of rich connection in the eyes of her daughters. It helped her to establish an inward stability reflected in the home they shared. But now, in the space that imbued her life with security, she only experienced an overwhelming sense to leave, move, get out...*now!*

The urgency in which the sensation coursed through her body left her off-kilter as she stood up from the crossed-legged position of her meditation. Stella felt so dizzy that she collapsed back down on to the floor. She tried to gather herself by propping up on her hands and knees, but her strength failed her.

"Pack a bag, get the girls, and go," she whispered, as to give the plan confidence as well as her heart the courage to do what she feared most.

She needed to protect her family but as she rose, the weight of it all pushed her back down onto the ground once again.

"Where do I go? The girls aren't ready, I'm not ready." Her voice cracked from the fear building inside her. Then another overwhelming sense. This time she could actually hear the words on the edge of her consciousness call out to her. *GO...NOW.* Then again, *GO, NOW*. It became clear that the voice was familiar as it implored her to leave. She finally stood with the ground firmly under her feet and walked out of her bedroom.

The next thirty minutes flew by in seconds. Stella grabbed all that she could carry in two black duffle bags for herself and her girls. She then walked to a portrait on the wall of the three of them, pushed it aside to reveal a safe, entered in a code, and the door opened. Inside was a small five-by-eight leather-bound notebook and a 9mm handgun with bullets. She put them carefully into the bottom of one of the duffle bags and loaded them into her jeep.

When she re-entered her home her daughter's artwork framed a sign in the entry that read, "Family, No One is Left Behind." Asante's vibrant depictions of waves of varying sizes crashing on a shoreline captured Stella's breath. In the living room, signs of Aissa's budding curiosity and imagination were illustrated in the intricate block cities that she built. Her daughters were more than she ever hoped they would be and yet still so young. Her sense of protection became an armor around her frightened heart, informing her steps as she walked down the hall to the girls' bedroom.

"Asante, Aissa," she whispered in the glow of the dawn's early light streaming into the girls' room across their sleeping faces. Though they each had their own twin sized bed, Aissa would get up in the middle of the night to sleep with her sister. Her little body was wrapped around Asante when Stella sat at the edge of the bed.

"Momma," Asante answered as she opened her eyes, "Is it time for school already?"

She did not want to alarm the girls, so she lied. "No, but we are getting up early to go on a special field trip to the zoo. And guess what, sissy poo can come too!"

"Ok, Mommy." Asante's voice was thick with sleep. "But Aissa has to listen to me because I'm older, so I'm in charge!" The idea of any of them being in charge of anything at that moment made Stella laugh nervously. But it gave her pause as well. They had been running for years until Asante was of school age and the last two years had been good to them. Safe, hidden, normal. What if she was wrong and she was to destroy the tiny bit of certainty she had established since Michael? Ok, she decided one last family breakfast in their home and then they would go.

2

She kissed both girls and asked, "Who wants pancakes, sleepy heads?"

At this, Aissa shot straight up in the bed and with her arm stretched as far as her fingers would pull, screamed "I Do. Me, me!"

"Asante, get dressed and help your sister as well and meet me in the kitchen in ten minutes for some strawberry jacks!"

"C'mon Aissa, I'll let you have the biggest one if you hurry up and let me pick out what you are going to wear," Asante encouraged Aissa as they hopped out of the bed. Stella left the room and walked back down the long hallway, passed the living room to the kitchen, with tears in her eyes.

When she got there, she wiped her face and looked around, but it was as if she had never seen it before. For a moment she did not know where anything was located. All she felt was panic, the sight of her innocent children brought the gravity of what was at risk to her full attention, the rest of her mind was in a fog. She took a deep breath and broke it down into steps.

"Bowl," she whispered to herself. She then opened a cabinet to her left and found the bowls. Grabbed one of the appropriate sizes and put it on the counter. "Pan," then without thinking she bent down to another set of cabinets and found her pots and pans, she took one out and placed it on the stove. Stella continued with this process until she had all the elements to make the pancakes. She began to whisk the batter while she tried to work out in her head where they would run. She had been devising a contingency plan for months, but nothing was solid. Her contact at the Eslan Institute had not written back to her in weeks...*is that how they found us?*

"Mommy!" Shouted the girls, interrupting her thoughts. Asante and Aissa sat at the table and stared at her in awe.

She looked down at her hand to find she was pouring pancake batter on the counter instead of the hot frying pan adjacent.

"Oh Shit," Stella said jumping slightly back and into the moment. "Mommy must need more coffee," she laughed as she began cleaning the mess on the counter.

Asante asked, "Are you ok, Mommy?" looking at her with worry in her eyes.

Determined to distract her girls, Stella answered, "Yes sweet face, are y'all ready for the zoo! Which animals do you want to see most?"

"The giraffes, the giraffes!" Aissa squealed.

"I want to see the lions," Asante replied as she seemed to drift off into thought. *Could she feel it too,* Stella wondered? The fear in her body flooded to her eyes and she began to sob over the stove. Both girls rushed to her sides and she bent down to embrace them and kiss their little faces.

"Mommy, you don't have to make pancakes if you're too tired," little Aissa whispered into her hair as she held them tight. *GO, NOW!* She knew it in every fiber of her being as she released them.

"Ok girls, let's do Mckie D's on the way to the zoo. I'll get a large coffee and we'll get two big pancake breakfasts for my two big girls! Get your jackets," Stella grabbed her keys and bag, took one more look at their home and ushered the girls out the front door. As they descended the steps the girls began to sing the, "Ready for the Day," song that she taught them.

With each step, the pit of Stella's stomach hollowed the confidence she was so desperately trying to establish. Something was wrong. Something that she couldn't perceive as though it was specifically placed in her blind spot. She felt like she was walking into a trap but like a moth to a flame, it couldn't be helped. As she looked down at her girls, holding hands and singing, she hoped that the fire that was coming wouldn't consume them as well. She hoped for their future, she hoped for her past, she hoped for the world. She would give her last breath to ensure their fate.

As they reached the sidewalk, Stella looked up and down the street several times. Nothing. Silence. They walked toward the jeep.

When they got to the Jeep Cherokee she fumbled with the keys as her hands shook almost uncontrollably. Asante looked up at her again with worry in her eyes. Stella smiled as reassuringly as she could. Days filled with laughter and light engulfed her mind's eye as she met Asante's gaze. *They need you, move, Stella, now.* She steadied her heart, then her hands, finally she opened the door and let Asante in. She then grabbed Aissa's hand and walked around the back of the jeep to put her in the car on the opposite side. Stella looked down the street. Nothing. Again silence. She opened the door and buckled Aissa in. As she closed the door, the lights of the 18-wheeler truck that sped toward her flooded her vision. They had found them. The truck side-swiped her jeep. Stella flew through the air from the impact as life began to leave her body. The truck never stopped and seemed to vanish as quickly as it appeared.

The sun continued to rise in the sky as the condensation on car windows evaporated. Birds, uninterrupted, sang their early morning melodies in the trees that lined the street. All was as it was a moment before. But the last sounds that Stella heard as the night of death crept into her consciousness were the cries of her two little girls. Their weeping tore through this otherwise picturesque morning as blood pooled around their mother's broken body, evidence that nothing would ever be the same.

Chapter 2
Asante

5:55 am, Asante opened her eyes and looked at her clock. Once again, she cheated herself out of the last five minutes of slumber before her alarm was to ring. Why was she always so "Ready for the Day"? She recalled the song of her childhood. This made her smile for a moment, but the water that stung her eyes quickly replaced her joy with pain from her heart that the memory brought back. She hadn't consciously thought of Stella and Aissa in over ten years. She had done quite well at compartmentalizing her tragic childhood in order to survive and since she gave up looking for her sister, that part of her life died. She rationalized that the double shifts at the hospital must be getting to her and got out of the bed.

Her twenty-five-hundred square foot penthouse apartment at the Paramount, overlooking San Francisco's breathtaking skyline, was a reflection of Asante's determination to not be defined by unfortunate circumstances. The décor, layout, and functionality of her space emulated her meticulous need for order and control. Nothing was out of place. She walked through her all-white home with pride and satisfaction until she reached the kitchen where her espresso waited for her, piping hot. As she sipped, she breathed in the aroma of the Columbian beans mixed with the Vanilla Orchid, which adorned her marble countertop. She made it, she was Dr. Asante Argueta, in control of her life and nothing would stop her.

In the shower, she began to mentally go through her day which she memorized the night before as she fell asleep. *Eight am-- triple bypass surgery with Mr. Seager; fifty-five, ex-smoker, morbidly obese, diabetic, high-risk. Three-thirty pm--Heart Valve Replacement Consult with Miss. Garner; seventy-two, athletic, great health, low risk.* As she continued to review her cases, Asante's thoughts were interrupted by a vision of the eyes of Mr. Seager's daughter. Asante met with the family the day before for a consultation on today's procedure. The mixture of fear and love in the girl's eyes struck Asante in a part of her soul that she thought was lost.

Asante knew all too well the trauma of losing a parent, losing the security of home that one's family provided. Even with all of her accomplishments, a hidden void was within her that she wouldn't wish upon an enemy much less this young girl who somehow reminded Asante so much of herself. Her experience and training would not let her make a verbal promise, especially in light of such a high-risk case. But now standing under the hot water beating on her back, she decided that she would not lose Mr. Seager on the operating table today, no matter what.

"Good morning, Dr. Argueta," Massah, one of Asante's residents, greeted her as she entered her office at St. Mary's Presbyterian. "Are you ready for the day?"

Feeling as though she had been pushed out of her body momentarily, Asante snapped back "What did you say to me?"

Massah looked like she stepped in it, though not sure what she did wrong, and not wanting to displease her Attending. She stammered, "I...I just was asking if you were, ready for Mr. Seager, not that you wouldn't be...or are in any way unprepared, it was just a figure..."

"I misheard you," Asante assured her, as she cut her off as promptly as she could, realizing that she was the one being weird. Why was she so anxious and triggered again by that phrase? "Yes, I'm ready, meet you down there in twenty." Massah left promptly, not sure what to make of the interaction.

Two hours later, after Asante had cut through the pericardium and was to begin replacing the blocked arteries with the healthy blood vessels from Mr. Seager's leg, her fears materialized. Massah accidentally damaged two of the three healthy veins. It was a complete freak accident. She actually sneezed while handling them and cut them, leaving them unviable. Massah looked at Asante over her mask with tears and regret in her eyes.

Massah and the entire room began to fade away from Asante's view. The open chest cavity of Mr. Seager became all the more vivid from her perspective. She could feel the pumping of his blood through the bypass machine in her ears, sweat began to drip down her brow as she steadied her hands. Mr. Seager's life hung in the balance with only moments to define his fate. She felt her unspoken promise embody her being and then a rush of air blew into her ears. Her body quickened from the sensation as it startled her at first, but as she gave it more attention, the blowing only became stronger, almost willing her to act. In the midst of this wind with an unknown source, a complete peace and knowledge of what she must do came over her.

Asante picked up the first of the damaged arteries and moved toward Mr. Seager's chest. She could faintly hear Massah's protest.

"Dr. Argueta!"

Almost in a trance, Asante's turned to her and uttered, "You must have been mistaken Massah, everything is as it should be." She continued on with the surgery with the complete assumption that the arteries were whole and the bypass would work. She shut out any other possibility and worked with every part of herself from that desired end. A few minutes later Mr. Seager was taken off the bypass machine and checked. His heart was pumping on its own. Massah was in complete shock, questioning if she had actually damaged the healthy veins in the first place. What did she just witness?

Asante gave Massah a confident smile. She was happy but unaware of anything out of the ordinary. She celebrated with an inward sense of completion feeling satisfied in the knowledge that she kept her innermost promise. Nothing more, nothing less.

Stenciled in bronze letters on a large teak door read, "Dr. Brennan Valdis, Surgeon-In-Chief". Asante grinned to herself as she knocked, knowing why she had been summoned to the preverbal principal's office. She had been a bad girl.

"Come in," She heard a rich baritone voice say from inside the office. She entered.

"Dr. Valdis," the words dripped from her lips.

"Dr. Argueta, close the door." He came from around his large teak desk and stood squarely in front of her. He was a good foot taller than she and his green eyes pierced hers as he grabbed her. They embraced while he kissed her lips with aggression yet coupled with gentle precision. He literally took her breath away. Asante smiled, her dimples creased into the depths of her cheeks as they separated. "Why haven't I seen you in seventy-two hours and we work in the same hospital?" He inquired.

"Did you really call me here to look at my pretty face?" She bantered back.

"That's not the only reason, I called you here." His tone changed. "Tell me about the Jared Seager case."

"Well, he's two days post-op, recovering nicely from what my residents tell me. Why?" Asante was genuinely curious. Brennan searched her face for any tells.

"Well, speaking of your residents, Massah David had a very interesting story about what happened in the operating room." There was a long awkward pause, while they both waited for the other to speak. Brennan broke the silence, "What's your explanation?"

"I'm sorry, an explanation for what?" Asante retorted with clear indignation.

"For using what appeared to be damaged veins in a bypass surgery?" He seemed to lose his temper a bit. His coloring changed as tiny beads of sweat broke out on his forehead.

"They weren't damaged." Asante shot back.

"How do you know? Did you examine them?"

"I don't recall, is there a problem here?" Asante began to feel uncomfortable and shifted in her stance. Again, Brennan seemed to be searching her face for something. Another long silence stretched the distance between them.

"Actually, no. The real reason, I called you here is Seager turns out to be loaded and made a five million dollar donation to the Cardiology Department this morning." Brennan offered.

"Wow, that's generous!" Asante smiled through her teeth, although she felt like she was outside of her body and was going to be sick upon hearing this news.

"Well, the board would like to thank you personally and Fairchild himself wants to hold a dinner at his estate this Saturday night in your honor!"

The pit of Asante's stomach began to churn with fear. She was confused by the reaction within herself but disregarded it, instead smiled and said, "I'll be there. Will you be my date?"

"Of Course, I'll pick you up at seven thirty." He looked down at her and they embraced once again.

The feeling in her stomach intensified. Asante had to get out of there. "I have a consultation in thirty." She lied. "I got to go, I'll call you later," her voice trailed behind her as she rushed out of his office.

After his door closed. Dr. Valdis picked up his cell phone and texted a number he entered manually from memory. *Saturday is confirmed. No awareness of what she has done. It'll be such a waste if you are wrong.* He pressed send. Then deleted the message from his phone.

Chapter 3
Asleep

The sound of computer keys clicking as the social worker typed up the case for Asante and Aissa echoed in Asante's mind. It drowned out all the other noise of the busy police station. Officers occupied themselves with paperwork, interviewing witnesses, and questioning perpetrators throughout the station. No one noticed that their world had just been torn apart.

Asante was cold and frightened as she held her little sister's hand who rocked back and forth in her chair as she hummed. The left side of Aissa's face above her eye had bandages, she stared at something that Asante couldn't see. She didn't know exactly what was wrong with her sister, but the glass from the jeep window seemed to have cut more than just Aissa's face. However, Asante did know their lives would never be the same. *Momma is...gone.* The thought of it made her tremble. *How could she be gone? What will they do with us?* It had just been the three of them. Asante hadn't seen their dad since Aissa was in Mommy's tummy. She was four then but had stopped asking about him when her mother's answer never changed. "I don't know where Michael is, but I hope we see him again one day," she would say.

"My name is Mrs. Oberland." Asante was brought back to the present. A silver-haired, pale skinned, very slender white woman with an extremely long neck sat across from Asante and Aissa. "I am a social worker and I help children like you get settled again when their world gets turned upside down, do you understand?" Asante, nodded yes, Aissa continued to hum and rock. At this, Mrs. Oberland directed her questions to Asante. "What is your name honey?"

"Asante Argueta." she nearly whispered.

"And your sister?"

Asante cleared her throat, "Aissa Argueta."

"How old are you and your sister?" Mrs. Oberland asked.

"I'm almost seven, my birthday is July thirty-first, and my sister is four, she just had a birthday, March eleventh."

"Wow, she's tall for four and you are quite articulate for almost seven."

"Thank you," Asante replied.

"Can you tell me about what happened this morning? What happened to your mother?" Mrs. Oberland asked cautiously. Asante shook her head *no*.

"Your neighbor, Mrs. Morrow, said she heard a crash and then you and your sister's screams. She said when she looked outside her window all the cars were parked along the street including yours, but your mother was faced down in the street some fifteen feet from your jeep. No other cars were seen leaving the scene. Mrs. Morrow then called nine-one-one and came to see about you and Aissa. She was with you until the police arrived. Did a car hit your mother, Asante, what did you see?"

Asante's stomach started to feel as it did the last time she looked into her mother's eyes. Like snakes slithering from the inside out. Her forehead broke out in a sweat and her body went from cold to hot very quickly. She thought of the last moments of her mother's life and it all seemed unimaginable. *A big truck appeared out of thin air, hit my mother, then vanished as quickly as it came. Isn't that what I saw?* She once again shook her head 'no' and began to stare at the ground.

"Do you know of anyone who wanted to hurt you or your mommy?"

Asante looked up, wide-eyed. Up until that moment she had assumed it was some type of accident, although she couldn't explain the truck. She began to replay the morning's events in her mind. "Mommy was scared!" It slipped out of her mouth before she could hold it in. Mrs. Oberland looked at her intently.

"Scared of what, Asante?"

"I don't know." She responded. Asante put her hand over her mouth and started to cry. Mrs. Oberland got up, came around the desk and hugged Asante's limp frame.

"Uh-hum," A tall man in a scruffy brown suit approached the desk. "Excuse me, Sheila." At this, Mrs. Oberland stood up and stepped away from them.

Aissa began to hum louder, making it hard for Asante to hear. "Shhh, Aissa," Asante whispered. Aissa didn't listen and continued to hum.

Asante then heard *"hit and run,"* a moment later, *"No family."* Aissa continued to hum even louder. Asante held her hand to grab her attention but this time noticed Aissa's hand was even warmer than her own. Startled she touched Aissa's forehead, it burned like fire. She was about to call Mrs. Oberland back over but she and Mr. Brown Suit had returned.

"Mrs. Oberland, my sister..."

"Asante, listen to me," Mrs. Oberland interrupted her in a tone that immediately got Asante's attention. "This is my associate, Mr. Douglas. We just want to confirm; do you have any family that you could stay with?"

Asante quickly answered, "No." Something was wrong, the snakes had returned to the pit of her stomach and Aissa's hand was getting hotter.

"Well, Mr. Douglas has been trying to find a family where both of you can stay temporarily until a proper foster family can be established. However, there doesn't seem...Aissa, honey can you quiet down," Aissa was so loud that the rest of the station seemed to hush and be looking in their direction. Aissa kept humming, Asante's hand started to hurt. "Anyway, we are going to have to separate you, just temporarily, until we can find you a home together, now say your goodbyes."

"But Mrs. Oberland I think my sister is sick, she's burning up!" However, Mrs. Oberland couldn't quite hear her over Aissa's piercing hum. Asante let go of Aissa because it felt like her hand was actually on fire. As she looked down to check it she noticed Aissa's chair was shaking and now so were the objects on Mrs. Oberland's desk. Aissa screamed and at that moment a jolt shook the entire police station. All the glass in the police station shattered at once.

Someone screamed, "Earthquake, take cover!" File cabinets tipped over, while objects flew everywhere. The ground beneath Asante's feet moved as if it were a rolling wave, she looked at Aissa, who continued to scream but the rest of her body was still. Asante tried to get closer to her when she was thrown to the ground by a desk that had shifted. The blow to her head knocked her unconscious for a few moments. When she opened her eyes, her head thundered with pain.

Although her vision blurred, Asante could sense the chaotic scene that swept the police station. She barely could make out her sister who sat calmly in the midst of it all. That's when Asante noticed Mr. Douglas, who was about ten feet from Aissa staring at her. But as the earth moved under his feet, his body seemed to absorb the movement so it appeared as though he moved with it. He walked toward Aissa in a straight line. He stood right behind her and grabbed Aissa's head, then he put his arms around her neck in a choke hold until she lost consciousness.

"No, Aissa," Asante whispered. The shaking stopped. Asante couldn't keep her eyes open. She fell asleep.

When Asante woke, she could feel the vibration of the tires against the road. The smell of leather on the hot seat she lay upon mixed with blood from her head. She was in the back of a car. Alone. Her head ached as the scene at the police station floated back into her mind. *Aissa!* Her vision still was a bit blurry as she tried to focus on the car door handle. After a few moments, she pulled herself up in the seat to find Mrs. Oberland in the front driving. "Where is my sister?" Asante's voice cracked.

"Your sister is safe and so are you," She continued, "What an earthquake! We're lucky that we weren't really hurt, although you did hit your head pretty bad. Go back to sleep and get some rest, we still have a while yet until we arrive at the Hughes Home for Girls. They have nurses there on staff, we'll get your head looked at."

"But where is my sister?" Asante asked again. A question that would go unanswered.

Chapter 4
Awakening

The yellow diamonds in Asante's tennis bracelet dazzled each time they passed a street lamp. The refraction of light lit up the back of the town car that she and Brennan rode in toward Mr. Fairchild's estate in the uber-luxurious Presidio Heights. Brennan smiled at her as he touched her wrist and admired the gift he had given her a year ago. "You are stunning."

She smiled back in return but felt uneasy inside. She had not been able to shake the agitation that entered her stomach since she was in his office two days ago. Although she never actually met Fairchild, she didn't think it was nerves. The feeling was vaguely familiar but she couldn't quite place it.

She looked out the window to distract herself. She met her own reflection, her perfectly shaped almond, almost black eyes, were wild with curiosity. Her waist length hair; pinned up and framed her caramel skin perfectly. Her make-up was flawless, however, all she felt was exposed.

She forced her attention to the beautiful aesthetic that her eyes encountered beyond the window. She had never been to this part of San Francisco, the homes were massive. Regal almost. They turned onto Maple Street and as they pulled into the private cul-de-sac driveway, the ground lights that illuminated the Georgian style estate looked so ominous that she laughed out loud at the fear building inside her.

"What's so funny?" Brennan asked curiously.

"I'd just thought it would be bigger." They both laughed together taking in the fifteen-thousand square foot home.

The car stopped. The door opened. And standing outside in a black well-tailored suit was an extremely tall man, at least a half foot taller than Brennan, who was six-two.

"Dr. Valdis," He greeted Brennan as he stepped out of the car and shook his hand.

"Carmichael, good to see you," He then reached back into the car for Asante's hand.

"May I present, Dr. Asante Argueta," she stepped out of the car and stood between both men who towered over her five-foot-three frame. "This is Carmichael, Mr. Fairchild's right hand."

"A pleasure to meet you, Carmichael," She charmed. He smiled warmly, but his eyes took in every inch of her black lace, Dolce & Gabbana, knee length cocktail dress with the hunger of a wild beast. She shuttered in response. *What is with me, shake it off, Asante*, she admonished in her self-talk. She wasn't usually so reactive to people.

As they followed Carmichael into the house, Asante locked arms with Brennan and pulled herself closer to him to whisper, "I didn't know that you and Fairchild knew each other so well that you're intimate with his personal staff, how many times have you been here?"

"Once or twice," he casually replied, but somehow Asante felt confident he was lying to her.

They walked into an opulent high ceiling foyer at the center of which hung the most enchanting crystal chandelier Asante had ever encountered. Beams of light reflected off the cream walls. The double grand staircase gave the entrance a palatial quality. As they walked under it and entered a burgundy velvet wall-papered, mahogany-paneled corridor, Asante felt like she left the twenty-first century and traveled back in time. The sitting room in which they entered was decorated impeccably. Gold and burgundy accents adorned most of the furniture. Yet it was all so incredibly masculine that it could have doubled as a smoking lounge in some old country club. She had expected to see some doctors or board members from the hospital, but she only recognized one of the twelve or so faces that seemed to simultaneously turn and look at them as they entered.

Mr. Fairchild's beady eyes filled with delight at seeing her. A wide smile on his portly face greeted her before they actually approached.

All of a sudden, her stomach lurched, the feeling of snakes writhing in her gut erupted from the pit of her bowels. She remembered all too clearly now the last time she had felt this type of sensation in her body. The day she had lost her mother and Aissa. The hairs on the back of her neck rose as he reached for her hand. Before she could fully process what she was feeling, he grasped her hand in his and drooled, "I'm so glad the occasion has risen for us to finally meet."

She felt a large lump in her throat when she tried to speak. She forcibly cleared her esophagus, took a deep breath and answered, "The pleasure is all mine, Mr. Fairchild."

"Please, call me Eric, may I call you Asante?" As he said her name, she instinctively began to search the room for exits. Her flight intuition had been triggered. But in her panic, she couldn't see any exit from her vantage point other than the corridor in which they had entered. She began to question herself. Asante hadn't noticed any other doors or entryways in the foyer. She had the unsettling feeling she was missing something very important. She began to feel warmth emanate from the writhing snakes in her gut. *Asante!* Again her inner rational began to speak to her. *You are ok, this dinner is in your honor, though strangers, these people are here because of your work. Calm down.* This seemed to slow her racing heart. *Drink,* she thought.

"Of course, Eric," she replied in a beguiling fashion. There were two waiters with glasses of champagne on trays. She overtly eyed one of them and Fairchild took the bait.

"Champagne?" he suggested, waiving the waiter over to where they stood.

"Yes, please," She said all too quickly. She grabbed the glass and didn't wait, she downed over half of it in a moment. Fairchild and Brennan looked at her nervously.

"Are you feeling ok?" Brennan leaned in and touched her elbow slightly. She smiled at him assuredly and turned her attention back to Fairchild.

He stared at her so intently, almost as if he were in search of something. *What is he looking for?* She finally assumed that she was just overwhelmed with it all and decided her overworked mind was playing tricks on her and dismissed her instincts.

He seemed to sense this in her and gently took her other elbow in his hand and began to guide her across the room and started with, "I know that you expected to talk with the members of the board tonight and hear our words of appreciation for the incredible work you've done, especially the latest surgery garnering such a generous donation to the hospital."

"Something like that, mixed with a little 'Eyes Wide Shut' action actually," she interjected.

He smiled and looked as though he was holding back laughter. "Beauty and wit, a lethal combination," He retorted. "One which I felt was better suited for talking to the powers that be behind what we really do. The money, the private investors that fund our endowment for our little healing center." He smiled.

"How altruistically plutocratic of you?" She joked a bit, testing the waters.

"Judge me after you see what we can accomplish together." He whispered nearly into her shoulder.

At this, they had reached a slender woman dressed as though she were a character in a nineteen-twenties film. She was actually smoking what seemed like a Virginia slim in a long silver cigarette holder. Her skin looked alabaster juxtaposed her illustrious raven colored hair. She smelled of mint and rosemary. She held out her gloved hand which Fairchild held and kissed. "May I introduce Dr. Elouise Schmidt, Chair of The Quanta Foundation. Dr. Asante Argueta."

"How incredible to meet you, Dr. Argueta. I hear your work isn't short of miraculous and that you have a very bright future." She almost sang in a thick German accent.

"I wouldn't know about miracles but thank you. I'm afraid I know nothing of your work, what is your focus at the Quanta Foundation?" Asante barely managed, not wanting to display her amusement at Dr. Schmidt's voice, cadence, and general appearance.

"To explore possibility and fund that exploration in corporations, start-ups, individuals, pretty much anywhere we see fit."

How vague, Asante thought, yet she felt like it was a clue to the *something* that she had missed. "So where do your interests lie with St. Mary's Presbyterian?" She asked.

"There will be time to discuss all of that later, for now, let's just say, she's here for you." Fairchild offered, as he once again took her elbow and started to guide her toward a couple standing near one of the large windows looking out at the skyline.

Asante heard Elouise to her back say, "So nice to have met you!"

"It was nice meeting..."

Fairchild stopped her, "She knows my dove, she knows."

Dove, is he for real? Asante thought. *I hope he didn't take my Eyes Wide Shut joke literally.*

Her attention immediately shifted as they approached the man and woman in the window. The couple did not captivate Asante, but the city behind them. Asante rubbed her eyes.

"Hi, darling, I'm Adele Vanderneiss and this is my husband, Ethan Vanderneiss. It's a pleasure to make your acquaintance." She held out a hand dripped in jewels.

Asante tried to focus on the woman in front of her, but the city. Her eyes began to water, it was so beautiful, but she didn't know what sprawled before her. Fairchild was saying that the Vanderneiss' were founders of the parent company that owned three of the largest television networks in the United States, Transverse Media.

As she continued to stare out the window his voice got further and further away from her conscious mind. It looked like Northern Lights but instead of moving and emanating in the clouds and sky, the lights' beautiful hues of purples, pinks, green and blue, seemed to be moving inside the city, on and in between buildings. Almost as if it came from the ground up. What's more is that she felt as though the movement of the lights were somehow connected to her, like she could sense them in her own body.

"I'm—I'm sorry..." she tried to return to the room, "Do you guys see what I see?" She stammered and pointed out of the window at the dancing lights.

The Vanderneiss' turned to look out the window, then in sync, very slowly, they turned to look back at her, their eyes bright with excitement.

They do see it, she thought, relieved she wasn't going crazy. Then, "It's working, Eric," Ethan said almost greedily.

"What's working?" Asante asked as she turned to look at Fairchild. *Have they drugged me?* She immediately thought of the champagne. *Had anyone else drunk from that tray of glasses? No, not even Brennan. Where is Brennan?* Her legs felt as though they would give out and then she almost lost her footing as Fairchild's face came into view.

The contorted look of pure darkness was illuminated in his countenance and his pupils expanded to make his eyes appear completely black. "Yes, it seems as though the compound is working, a bit quicker than we expected. So, let's assess what she can do, not just see!" Fairchild's voice deepened.

Air began to rush into Asante's ears again as if someone were blowing into them. The same sensation from the operating room had returned. *Run, Go…Run Now!* She felt it so clearly that it almost seemed audible. She listened. She turned to run toward the corridor in which they had entered. But now there were three men and Carmichael running out of it headed straight for her. She tried to outmaneuver them by using her lower center of gravity to her advantage when she was grabbed from behind.

She could tell it was Brennan immediately from his cologne. "Don't fight!" He pleaded into her ear as he tightened his grip across her chest. But that's exactly what she did. She elbowed him in the stomach and was about to break free when she felt more hands on her body, wrestling her to the ground.

She began to fight back with every ounce of her being. They couldn't hold her down, she knew it, she was more powerful than these five men. She became acutely aware that the strength she embodied was not a physical one. Asante could sense where each one of their focus and energy was in relation to her body before actual contact. At that moment she was as malleable as the best contortionist and as agile as Bruce Lee. Every time they seemed to have control of her, she became more and more elusive until she managed to free herself of them completely. The men continued for a moment in a pile of arms, legs, and bodies before they realized she was running away from them.

Asante was amazed by what she had just accomplished but had no time to take it in. She was just about to exit the burgundy corridor as she felt a pinch to the left of her shoulder blade. She fell forward and reached behind herself to find an object protruding from her back. They shot her with something. She rolled over onto her side as she felt a cold numbing liquid travel from the point of impact and spread throughout her body. She lost feeling in her limbs as she looked up at the enchanting crystal chandelier of the foyer. It was still beautiful. The cold had reached her head, her vision blurred to black. She lost consciousness.

Chapter 5
Obadias

"Any Change?"

"She's still asleep."

"The dose of Respirodol might be too heavy, she's been this way for a day and a half."

"Nope, doc, says she's dangerous and the best way to get back from a psychotic break is rest."

"Shame, she's a beauty, surgeon I heard?"

"Yep, guess the stress got to her."

Asante listened with her eyes closed to the nurses changing shifts in her room. She actually woke up in the middle of the night, realized she was in restraints, which frightened her, but she quelled her instinct to scream out because the memory of what happened before she was obviously sedated flooded her mind. She desperately grasped at a notion of certainty, but the assumption she settled on was that she was in some type of mental health facility from the restraints and now the knowledge of what medication had been making it hard for to maintain consciousness. *What in the hell was going on?*

Asante then heard the door to her room open. "Dr. Farraday," the nurses called out in unison.

"You can leave us," a raspy female voice replied. The door closed and then she heard several high heeled steps come closer to where she lay. She felt someone sit at the edge of her bed near her waist and touch one of her restrained hands gently. "Dr. Argueta," the same raspy voice questioned with expectation.

Asante opened her eyes slowly. Before her, sat a very attractive blonde short-haired girl. At least she appeared to be no more than fifteen. But the nurses clearly called her doctor and she sounded as if she were a fifty-year-old, two pack a day smoker. Yet the most innocent set of doe eyes looked into Asante's soul.

"I am Dr. Emily Farraday. I am your Psychiatrist here at Gateway Health. You've been diagnosed with bipolar disorder based upon your erratic, manic, and dangerous behavior forty-eight hours ago at The Fairchild Estate." She paused here as she searched for a reaction in Asante's countenance. A moment later, "I want to be clear. I know, that both you and I know, that you are NOT bipolar and are NOT suffering from a psychotic episode due to the stresses of your career." Again Dr. Farraday paused for effect or inquiry, Asante couldn't decipher. "But know, I will never, under any circumstance testify to anything but the contrary. Now that I have been clear—everything I'm about to assert to you will be of your own volition to accept. We know who you are, who your family is, and what bloodlines you come from dating back several centuries. But what is still unknown to us is what your capabilities are. Although, we have been following your life closely for several decades, you were off-grid before we were able to locate and successfully separate you from your family. That being said, we've never been able to be sure of what information or talents your parents made you aware of before we got our hands on you."

Asante's eyes began to well with water as the gravity of this teen-woman's words hit her heart. Although the story she had just been told sounded like the prologue of a science fiction novel, a very dormant, oppressed, and scared part of Asante knew the truth.

The therapy she received at the Hughes House for Girls convinced her rational self that what she experienced the last time she'd seen her family was a post-traumatic stress response to being a witness to her mother's death. But in light of what she just heard and seen over the last week, she knew that what she thought possible, and what is actually real, are two very different things.

"We are not the enemy." Dr. Farraday continued, "Our only interest is in the preservation of humanity and we hope that you will voluntarily assist us in that effort."

"And what if I don't?" Asante spat as defiantly as she could muster.

"Dr. Argueta, Asante if I may, I repeat, WE are not the enemy. But make no mistake, we do feel like if you thwart our invitation to be a part of something that will positively impact the world we live in, then we may have to view you as one. Now I know that you have been through so very much and we don't want to put too heavy a burden on you at once. So the first thing I'm going to do is extend your seventy-two-hour, fifty-one-fifty hold to a thirty-day observation. You are too important to our work to rush this process.

We will be here for you every step of the way. Get comfortable, you're going to be here a while."

After the door closed, Asante began to sob. Fear had become tangible and she could feel it creeping into the entirety of her being. She was highly conflicted as well. Apart of her wanted to escape by any means necessary, though that same part felt her efforts would be futile in the end. Still, yet another part of her wanted to know more about the "We" Dr. Farraday spoke of. Was Fairchild at the helm? And what role did Brennan and the other "investors" she was introduced to play in all of this? And how had their "hands" been on her life, in what way? Asante's mind began to reel with query. She would only sleep three of the next eight hours and then wake at precisely 5:55 am.

She heard a knock at her door a few minutes later. "Good morning!" A bright, cheerful voice greeted her as the door opened. "I am Celia. I am the charge nurse on the west wing here at Gateway. So nice to meet you, Dr. Argueta! How are you feeling this morning?"

Was she in on it? Asante thought, *best not mention anything Dr. Farraday had said.*

"I'm tired, didn't sleep well," Asante responded.

"How odd, the medication we are giving you should be helping you to sleep as well as stabilize your mood. I'll tell Dr. Farraday and we'll make adjustments in a few days if it doesn't get better." Celia paused and looked at her quietly for a moment. *Here it comes* thought Asante.

"Now, Dr. Argueta." Genuine respect was evident in her voice, "Dr. Farraday has advised me that you have stabilized enough for you to come out of these restraints this morning and join the rest of the patients here."

"Come in," Celia shouted in a tone very different from what she had just been using with Asante.

Two very large men, who looked like security detail for some pop star, entered the room in all white. They stood silently on each side of Celia.

"I'm going to unbuckle these restraints now. After I do so, please slowly get out of the bed. Once you are sure on your feet, follow me out of the room and I will get you toiletries from the closet, sweats to wear, and show you where you can take a shower. Do you understand?"

Asante nodded.

"Also, no one here is going to call you Dr. Argueta. From here on out you will be addressed as Asante only, we don't want to confuse our other patients."

Asante followed Celia's instructions without the slightest variance. As they walked out into the hallway, Asante could immediately feel eyes on her. Patients hung out in the doorway of their rooms. Some stared at her with hollowed looks in their eyes, others with keen interest. They passed what looked like a cafeteria or gathering area as there were five to six round tables that looked as if they sat six to eight people each. Some patients were playing games, others were reading, some drinking coffee or tea. But some were having not so quiet conversations with themselves either at a window or wall. They finally reached a door that read "shower". Celia handed Asante toiletries, a towel, sweats, and slippers.

"Enjoy, you have five minutes."

The cold water hit Asante's face. She felt like she was waking up from a bad dream but knew all too well this wasn't the case. She spent many years in therapy "getting over" what happened to her sister and mother, but now all the anxiety she worked so hard at replacing with confidence was all that she could experience at the moment. In response, as if her mother could feel her vulnerability as if not bound by the laws of life and death, she heard her mother's voice singing in her head.

I am ready for the day, I am kind, I am brave. I'm exactly what I say, not tomorrow but today! I am ready for the day, night is gone, I'm awake. There is no time anyway, let's have fun and create. Don't delay, ride the waves, I am ready for the day. I am ready for the day, I am ready for the day. Goosebumps instantly sprung out all over her body. She got out of the shower ready for what lay ahead.

Over the next few days, Asante became accustomed to the routine she assumed would be her life until the powers that be saw fit to alter it. She kept her head down, besides greetings of salutation, spoke to no one. She hadn't seen Dr. Farraday but was reminded daily by the instructions left with Celia, that she was watching or being kept abreast of all of Asante's activity. Despite

Farraday's warning, Asante decided she would use her time wisely. She started creating lists of people, places, and experiences that might help to unravel the mysteries behind the unseen hand in her life. She would commit the information to memory, then at the end of the day, tear up the paper on which she wrote.

On about day five she noticed a new male nurse on the wing. At first, she didn't think much of him, just noted his presence and name, which was Obadias according to his nameplate. But by day eight, she was convinced he was spying on her. Possibly for Dr. Farraday who continued to be MIA.

The next day during the activity hour of arts and crafts, he was posted right behind her chair to supervise the group. He watched the group and seemed to be taking notes when he dropped a pen near her feet. They both bent down at the same time to pick it up. While they were on the floor he whispered "I know who you are, I'm here to help. Be ready," then he put his index finger over his mouth as to say, *don't speak*. They locked eyes and Asante nodded.

*   *   *

Obadias had been running up and down the same strip of Surf Rider's Beach at sunrise and sunset for as long as he could remember. But in his mind's eye, he visited some of the most beautiful horizons all over the world. He learned from a very young age that hidden was good, but hidden in plain sight was much better. His family had been successful in leading a very public life amongst a small group of people. Joshua and Jamillah Gotzon were retired successful pro surfers with a surf shop that they owned across the street from the beach in the Malibu Market. They rode the waves alongside Michael and Stella Argueta as they attempted to waken humankind to their potential in their youth. They were local living legends and great parents.

But Obadias was born with a thirst for more. He believed that although his family had definitely helped to raise the collective energy of their small town, the world was dying outside of this taste of paradise. It wasn't enough.

After his parents vanished, he kept his head down and ran the surf shop. He knew who was behind what he assumed was their demise, but nothing was to be done, not then. Instead, he indulged his imagination during his twice a day runs along the beach. There she ran alongside him, the girl of his dreams. *Aissa.*

Before his parents' disappearance, they were in search of Aissa and her sister, Asante. Joshua and Jamillah heard of their mother Stella's murder and wanted to save the girls. Although he'd only seen a worn-out Polaroid of Aissa as a toddler, he was connected to her. The leads his parents had on she and Asante dried up many years ago. However, he knew that he was destined to find them.

*   *   *

When Asante returned to her room that evening her mind was once again racing. Was this some type of test, what was Obadias' angle? "Ready for what?" She asked herself out loud in an incredulous tone. *This is crazy. The whole thing is nuts!* She didn't know who or what she was running from or who was trying to help her. But when she thought of Obadias air rushed into her ears again and she felt at peace. A knowing came over her to trust him. She decided she would, at least for now.

That night Asante lay awake replaying her interaction with Obadias over and over. She rolled onto her side and decided to get some rest, 5:55 am, the clock on her nightstand read. The door to her room opened and into the light from the hallway stepped Obadias. His finger was over his mouth again as he silently crept toward her.

"I need you to grab my hand and follow me. Do exactly as I say, when I say it. Do you understand?"

Asante thought *yes*, but, "No," came out of her mouth. "Where are we going, who are you?" She searched his eyes for the truth.

He looked at her, this time he was the one that looked scared. His eyes filled with water and a single tear rolled down his cheek. "I am here to save you but only because I know that you have already saved us all. The only other thing I can tell you right now is Aissa says, today, *I'm* in charge."

Asante's heart filled with so much joy that she barely noticed the rush of air blowing in her ears again. She had to go with this man even if it meant she may never see another day, the possibility of seeing her sister outweighed her own life.

He held out his hand, she grabbed it and followed him into the hallway. The nursing station was all the way down the hall, past the gathering area, right before the mechanical locked double doors to the wing. *How are we going to get past the nurses and operate the door with no one noticing? Even if the pass that hangs around his neck opened the doors, how will he sneak me out?*

He turned to her just then and whispered, "Move when I move, step where I step."

They moved down the hallway in the large shadows that were cast by every third light that was on. All the while Asante kept her eyes on the glass of the nurse's station. She could see that there were three nurses in there sitting at computers.

They had one more shadow to clear when Asante saw Celia get up and walk to the door of the station. It opened and she walked out directly across the hall to the medicine closet. She hadn't seen them but she surely would once she came out of the closet and came down the hall to whatever patient she was attending to.

Asante wanted to run back to her room, but Obadias held her hand tighter and pulled them forward. She heard the door click to the medicine closet, *she is coming.* At the last moment, he pulled her into the open door of a patient's room before the nurse's station and held his hand over her mouth.

Asante heard Celia walk by the room and down the hall, open a door, and say brightly, "Hello Mr. Highland, I have your Clonazepam." They had seconds.

As they stepped back out into the hall, Obadias raised his hand in the direction of the station and all the lights began to flash, the computer screens went blank as if they were all unplugged at once. Then all the lights in the hallway went out. The mechanical doors opened. He and Asante ran through, not looking back, she followed him down a series of hallways to a door that had a red exit sign above it. They rushed through it to find a staircase. They flew down the steps nearly a flight at a time. She thought they might tumble at any moment. They reached the ground level and opened the door.

She could see her breath in the cold early morning air. She was breathing, she was alive. Obadias reached for her hand again as she caught her breath. He turned her arm over so that the bandage where they had first administered her meds faced up. He then took out a knife, Asante flinched backward.

Obadias pleaded, "Trust me."

She reluctantly relaxed her arm. He then ripped the bandage off and made a small incision in its place in the crease of her elbow. A moment later a tiny blinking object was at the tip of his knife.

"What the hell?" Asante exclaimed.

"I know," he responded. "But there's no time, we've got to go on foot from here, my car is parked down the road but we must run now. They'll have a search team assembled in a half hour and we need to get off-grid."

They started to run.

Chapter 6
Running

Asante woke up at the sound of her own snoring. Obadias laughed. She took in his salt and pepper beard, caramel skin, and enormous eyes with the longest lashes she's ever seen on a man or woman. His salt and pepper roots spread perfectly through his not so manicured dreadlocks. She guessed he was about thirty from how youthful his face looked, besides his gray hair she didn't see any other evidence of aging, his perfect caramel skin, flawless. His gaze intently focused on the road.

He turned to her and said, "Are you feeling better, you knocked out pretty quickly after we got out of the city."

The forest lined highway they traveled was breathtaking, the sky was clear as the sun's rays lit up the vibrant powder blue horizon. However, Asante couldn't enjoy the view. She had fallen asleep with her mind racing. So many questions and emotions overwhelmed her at once. She was disoriented and frightened but more present then the fear was a sense that she had become more alive, more awake somehow. The center of her forehead felt like there was a gaping hole in it, almost as if something were being pulled out of her brain. Was she more aware or was she really having a psychotic episode? She was determined to find out.

"Yes, thank you," she finally answered. "And I mean for everything! But I do have some questions, I need some answers immediately," she demanded as the need to assert some control over her spun life rose from her gut.

"I'll do my best," he said.

"Where is my sister?"

"Outside the Mayacamas Mountains, on sacred native land, once inhabited by the Yukian Wappo Tribe. We are on our way there now. It's very tranquil. There are hot springs that soothe the body and relax the mind. It keeps her calm."

Calm?

"Has she been there all these years? How did she get there? How do you know her and what did you do with your hand to the nurse's station back at Gateway?" She rapidly fired, barely taking a breath between questions.

"I'll let your sister answer your questions for her but I will tell you about what I did at Gateway. However, first I'd like to ask you a question if I may?"

Asante nodded in response.

"What did you do during the Seagar operation at St. Mary's Presbyterian?"

"What, what does that have to do with anything?" She asked in disbelief.

"Everything. Please answer the question."

"I did a triple bypass. My resident thought there was a complication, that she had damaged some of the arteries accidentally, but…" she stopped speaking. She thought back to Brennan questioning her in his office a couple of days after the surgery. He was keenly interested in what she had done as well. *Brennan, damn,* Asante thought. Their relationship over the past ten years had been her only constant. She remembered struggling against Brennan and the others at The Fairchild Estate and felt sick to her stomach. *Is this another trap?* She looked at him for some modicum of evidence.

"But what?" He asked.

"But she was mistaken," she replied

"How do you know?"

"Because the bypass was a success. If the arteries were damaged, like my resident suspected, he would have died pretty quickly after we took him off the bypass machine. And as far as I know Mr. Seager is living his best life. Is there something you want to tell me? And how do you know about Seagar, anyway?"

"We hacked Brennan's computer to look at the footage."

"What footage?"

"Were you unaware that you worked in a teaching hospital?"

"No, of course not, but when we are being monitored for teaching, we are notified. Mr. Seagar's case wasn't recorded."

"Yes, it was," He pulled out his phone and pulled up a video. "Press play."

She began to watch. Within moments it was evident. Massah clearly damaged the arteries when she sneezed. They had to have been unviable. *So how did I...*

She looked at Obadias with wonder and disbelief. She started to feel cold, a chill literally ran up her spine.

"So, you didn't heal him on purpose?"

She didn't know how to answer that question, thinking of her inner promise.

Feeling like she was overwhelmed. Obadias said, "I will tell you what I did at Gateway."

Asante could see the compassion in his eyes.

"There's a theory that all living things are connected in some way to every part of the universe. Do you agree that in some way this is possible?"

"Yes, of course, on a molecular level," Asante agreed.

"Well, what if I told you that there is a conscious access point to that connection?"

"I'm listening." She had to have an open mind at this point.

"Are you familiar with brainwave entrainment?"

"Something about tuning the mind to a desired frequency either audibly or with light?"

"Yes, or a combination of both to induce the mind into a desired state. Either meditative, creative, analytical, etcetera," he continued. "What if I told you that the concept that brainwave entrainment points to is a secret ancient way of interacting with all the elements of this dimension. Instead of our brains being entrained by external stimuli like light or sound, our brains have the capacity to entrain the elements of the universe around us. We are the stimuli.

"What if I told you that this knowledge has been passed down through human history? That your ancestors were some of the few keepers of it on the planet. And that the women of your family were tasked with teaching the next generation as many of them were deemed alchemists, soothsayers, and witches.

"This ancient way teaches that when you are aligned with your highest vibration you become one with Source and the universe around you must bend to the induced state of your will. The access point to this vibration is through the present, '*The Now*' if you will. Some call it 'integration' but the point is that your highest potential is experienced.

"When the Bible spoke of man having dominion over this realm, it wasn't just a metaphor. This is what you saw me access this morning at Gateway, what you accessed unknowingly and quite remarkably while operating on Mr. Seagar and what you saw your sister access all those years ago in that police station."

"But how?" She asked, her mind racing at the possibility of what he had just said. *Aissa had caused that earthquake.* Asante was blown away.

"We're here," he responded as they turned off route twenty-nine onto a dirt road into the forest. A few moments later they reached a lake, drove around it until they were in front of a massive log cabin. Asante felt the blowing in her ears.

*   *   *

"Where are we?" Dr. Emily Farraday asked the room. Silence. She rose from her chair and stood in front of a wall filled with screens. Live and recorded footage were displayed on a few of them. However, most were filled with mug shot like pictures of individuals that were a priority for the day, along with real-time updates from sources all over the globe. All the screens turned black at once and only the face of Asante Argueta looked back at the room from the center screen.

"So, what you all would have me believe..." She continued, "by your lack of response, is that somehow this woman, who has no idea of the power she could potentially possess, has outmaneuvered our team at one of our high-level security facilities, then escaped, removed her tracker, mind you, that she had no knowledge of, and got off-grid in less than two hours? All by herself?"

Brennan looked around the conference table where he sat listening to Farraday. Though all the faces seemed somber at best, he was surrounded by some of the most powerful men and women in the world. The Council. He still couldn't believe that he had a seat. His father and grandfather before him had been members of The Sephiren. But they were never invited to have a seat at the table of the Council. With their help, he had spent much of his childhood attempting to unlock his own ability to entrain and integrate. However, it turns out, his cunning and wit were just as powerful as their physical manipulation of the elements, if not more. He had been working his way up the ranks of The Sephiren when he was assigned his golden ticket. Asante Argueta.

She had been one of his residents ten years ago and it felt like fate had brought them together. However, Brennan knew better. The reach of The Sephiren's manipulation on one's life was an ever-deepening rabbit hole. Every day there were new facets of their control being implemented over the general population but especially so of the individuals that were known by their case numbers. Asante was case #0143. By the time he met her, she was so eager to escape the pain of her childhood that she fell for him easily. It was effortless between them and Brennan had developed what he deemed as real feelings for her. He knew that she was unique but only recently was let in on how integral she was to the work of The Sephiren. Yet, he knew that he hadn't been given all the information about her. Farraday and Fairchild had secrets, but he hoped he could still somehow bring her into the fold despite this morning's events.

"Anyone?" Farraday asked again.

"Well, she might be fully integrated, look at how she responded to the compound within moments. We've never known someone to see through the veil that quickly." Adele Vanderneiss offered as more of a question than an answer.

Dr. Farraday smiled. "I understand your hope for zero-one-four-three, but we flushed the compound out of her body at Gateway and she showed no signs of integration. She reverted back to unsure and anxious, trying to establish the false sense of confidence that we helped to create in the first place." She paused and scanned the faces around the table. "I know there is evidence that she began to self-integrate—if there is such a thing—at the hospital during Mr. Seager's surgery but we don't know how or why. Yes, we do know the lineage from which she comes and what her sister is capable of but let us think this thing through." A long silence for a few moments, then she shouted, "Someone is helping her. Someone has been watching and waiting just as we have. The point is we need to find out now who it is, so we know what we are dealing with. Make her a level three priority on the grid...NOW!"

Chapter 7
Aissa

Aissa was scared because she knew at any given moment they would come for her again. The tests The Sephiren ran on her had become random. She used to be able to know when she could expect the next experiment. Tuesdays, they would take her into a room and lay her on a table that would move inside a large machine. There would be lights and sounds for her to experience but outside of that, no pain, no discomfort. She actually had grown accustomed to her time in the light and sound machine over the past eight years. She would imagine being reunited with her sister. She refused to believe that Asante died in the earthquake at the police station. The earthquake she would come to learn she had caused.

First, they taught her of integration. A word to describe being fully aware and aligned with any moment. *The Now.* It was an easy concept for her to grasp at four years old, without the distraction of television, school, organized religion or any other veil driven entity. They taught her techniques in meditation, Yoga, Tai Chi & Reiki to sharpen her awareness and alignment. The Sephiren also spent many hours teaching her about the world outside of the hospital. The world in which the masses lived. The grid. The world distorted by the veil. The knowledge that she was special and was here to protect humankind from their own folly had been drilled into her head daily. She was given a history of The Sephiren which dated back to Egyptian Civilization.

Then they taught her the science behind the entrainment of brain waves. It was an easy enough leap to understand how things actually worked with the human brain having the capability to entrain the physical universe. To the degree that one is aligned with an object or element's frequency combined with one's level of integration would determine the depth of the entrainment. So she learned of the unique connection between her vibration while integrated and the frequency at which tectonic plates shift.

However, this knowledge, the tests, nor the intense brainwashing never erased the connection she had with her mother and sister. She sang their, "Ready for the Day," song as much as she could remember. And as she got older she was convinced that the song was a way of her mother communicating with her. As well as the key to her freedom.

But the drugs and the tests were becoming invasive and harder for her to manage. She wasn't sure how much more she could take. Her five-two frame only held a mere ninety-five pounds on her last birthday. The day her menstruation began. She caused a three-point-two magnitude quake due to the pain that was uncontrollable. The staff sedated her in time before she did any real damage to southern California but the earthquake was felt some fifty miles away. Since that day her care and tests took a more painful direction. They began to force her into higher and higher states of integration using pain as the catalyst. At the same time, they would tranquilize her. She figured this was done to disrupt the synapses in her brain, therefore, lessening the vibrational impact on the frequency which the tectonic plates aligned. This enabled them to experiment on her and not cause any major damage or alarm because the quakes she created in this drug-induced state were of your standard one-point-zero magnitude or less, which is experienced in California almost daily.

Aissa decided to give her restless mind a break, it was the middle of the night, they probably wouldn't return until morning. She began to sing what she remembered of their song. *"I am ready for the day, I am kind, I am brave, I'm exactly what I say, not tomorrow but today. Don't delay, ride the wave, I am ready for the day..."* She entered into a meditative state before falling asleep. She was at peace.

At 4:44 am Aissa woke in a sweat. She had a dream that The Sephiren had decided to kill her. She then heard the lock to her door release. Aissa thought of the words to the song. Someone entered the room and through her cracked eyelids, she could see the silhouette of a syringe in their hand. Panic gripped her breath. She looked at the clock again, still, 4:44 am. *They are going to kill me.* She began to sing their song in her mind, she could feel the warmth emanating from her energy center at the top of her head known as her crown chakra. Her bed, the nightstand, the desk and ground all began to move. The walls started to crack. Whoever had come to kill her lay on the ground in front of her as she stepped out of the bed and onto the moving floor. A light fixture had swung down from the ceiling killing him instantly. She stepped over his body and moved with the shaking of the building as if it were a part of her. Moments later she walked out of the front doors of the hospital and the devastation of what she had done was everywhere. Destruction had touched everything her eyes encountered and the ground was still rolling. She severed the connection. This was the first time she was able to turn it off consciously.

Tears flooded down Aissa's face as she took in the havoc of what would come to be known as the Northridge '94 Earthquake. She was twelve years old and a killer, this pervaded her consciousness while she wandered the desolate streets of LA.

In the past six years, life had been challenging for Aissa. Mostly because she needed to stay off-grid. Therefore she lived amongst the disregarded and forgotten of the City of Angels. She spent most of her time between shelters, beaches, and libraries. Aissa added to her knowledge of entrainment by studying the teachings of Jesus, Krishna, The Zoroastrian Kings, The Buddha, and the Kabbalah. Though these were all different spiritual doctrines they all pointed to one truth; humans are infinite, expressing themselves in time.

The weather was hardly ever intolerable and Aissa lived off the kindness of strangers fairly well. She also continued to sharpen her techniques of integration or staying present by meditating three times a day. She was ready for The Sephiren if they tried to come for her again.

This particular morning she was hopeful that her course would soon change and bring her to her sister. She could feel it. Though her search of the LA area and southern California for Asante had proven to be futile, Aissa knew Asante wasn't far.

She had been saving for a bus ticket to travel to Northern California. Specifically to the Eslan Institute. She could spend time there sharpening her mind as well as look for clues of other factions. The Sephiren had alluded to other factions during her time in their possession. However, finding any evidence of their existence was an unfathomable task to undertake. But her instincts told her she was close to finding a link, clue, something was about to change.

She dug her feet deeper into the sand, her tattered jeans frayed at the ankles, were wet from the incoming tide. As she meditated on Ecclesiastes 3:11, she thought of the universe that Source had planted in her mind. She envisioned the connections between all living things. She surveyed Surf Rider's Beach. A family of four were making sand castles. A little further away a group of teenagers were obviously smoking pot. But in the ocean was the real action.

Surfers were riding waves with a precision that always struck Aissa into awe. *Don't delay, ride the wave.* Aissa smiled to herself. Then she saw him. His wetsuit clung to his muscular torso like a superhero. His dreadlocks flying behind him as he came out of the funnel and rode the wave to completion. *Is he looking at me?* His gaze was obviously focused in her direction, but there was no reason for him to notice her. She was purposefully as undesirable as she could possibly manage. Yet now he was coming out of the water carrying his board and walking straight toward her.

Aissa wanted to get up and run, but so much of herself declared interest and trust in the man approaching her. He stood two feet from where she sat. She made herself as still as possible. Then she looked up slowly to meet his gaze and found the most beautiful eyes in his countenance.

He grinned and said, "I am Obadias Gotzon, Aissa, I have ridden the wave to come meet you, will you have me?"

Aissa stood up and they embraced, she began to cry in the knowledge that she was no longer alone.

Chapter 8
Marie

The wind blew Aissa's curly hair as she clung for dear life to Obadias as they sped down the Pacific Coast Highway on his Harley. The sun was setting into a beautiful bouquet of violets, corals, and pinks that it captured her breath. She was at peace for the first time since she'd been with her mother and sister all those many moons ago. In the distance, a new moon was rising and Aissa took this as a sign. A symbol of what lay ahead.

She and Obadias had spent the entire day talking on the beach. He told her stories of The Wave, the faction that he belonged to, the faction that her mother, Stella, and father, Michael had given their lives and freedom for. He told her of how his parents had fought alongside them against The Sephiren and other sub-factions that were oppressing mankind. He said that he and the other members of The Wave had been searching for her and Asante since The Sephiren murdered their mother.

The motorcycle slowed grabbing Aissa's attention. They turned off Pacific Coast Highway and onto Sunset Boulevard and followed the signs that said Pacific Palisades. A few more turns and hills and they pulled up to a beautiful modern wood home surrounded by trees. It reminded Aissa of a tree house. There was a wooden bridge that went from the street to the entryway of the home. On each side of the bridge, a stream with large koi, ducks, and turtles as its inhabitants flowed.

As they got off and began to unload Aissa's few belongings from the storage compartment on the back of the bike, the large wooden double doors of the entryway opened. A svelte, long-legged, curly-haired, blonde girl, with caramel skin, came running out and across the bridge to meet them.

"Aissa," she seemed to scream at the top of her lungs, with her arms stretched out as wide as her fingers would pull. She came in for the real thing and immediately hugged Aissa so tight that she nearly lost her breath.

"I feel like I've been waiting to meet you my whole life, my name is Marie," she whispered in Aissa's ear as she held her. Aissa finally relented and released her body into the love that felt so much like home instantly. They walked hand in hand like little girls into the house.

The wood theme continued into the open floor plan home. Sitting at a fireplace were a group of what looked like members of an alternative rock band. Vibrant colored dyed hair, ripped jeans, plaid shirts in varied colors, and doc martens were adorned by all of them. In the kitchen was a woman cooking what smelled like heaven to Aissa. Aissa was introduced first to her. She had long silver hair to her butt. Eyes that mirrored Marie's of the clear aquamarine hue.

Marie said, "This is my Grandmother NikkiNicole."

She held out a hand, her wrist full of charms, and bracelets of every metal possible. "It's a pleasure to meet you Aissa, you have been blessed with your mother's beauty, both inside and out I'm sure!"

Aissa, shook her hand as her heart felt like it would implode with love and light. Aissa, responded with, "Will you tell me more of my mother?" This surprised Aissa, but NikkiNicole seemed to expect it and nodded while patting her hands as the words tumbled out of her mouth.

From the kitchen, they walked into a living space that flowed into an open garden with a spectacular view of the ocean. In the large door frame stood a girl wearing butterfly wings, with lavender hair, black ripped jeans, and fluffy pink slippers. She was a tad more timid in meeting Aissa but the warmth and love emanating from her matched Marie and NikkiNicole's.

"I'm J.StaRR, nice to meet you Aissa," she opened her arms slowly to embrace her. Aissa let go of Marie's hand and as she went to hug J.StaRR, there was a physical current between the two of them which she could feel in her whole being immediately. As they got closer a blue light became visible and began to emanate from their bodies. Obadias stepped in and pulled them apart.

"I thought that might happen," he turned to Aissa, "You and J.StaRR are alike in many ways. Like you, she's aligned with the frequency of tectonic plates. But she also has complete mastery over sound waves as well. She can actually manipulate the cells in our bodies with the pitch, tone, and vibrato of her voice."

Aissa's eyes opened wide with amazement.

The kids near the fireplace now walked over to where they stood and collectively introduced themselves, "We are The Misfitz!"

"This is my band," J.StaRR continued, "They share the same relationship to sound as I do with my voice but they can transmute it through the instruments they play. Eddie, Mystro, Chase Money, and Kaz." They all smiled and did a simultaneous bow. Aissa's heart soared.

After dinner, they all sat around a fire-pit beyond the garden, near a cliff. The ocean air combined with the company continued to imbue Aissa with peace.

In the midst of the tranquility Obadias began, "Aissa, we've yet to tell you what Marie's very special gift is. She's a telepath who writes and draws what she is able to see and hear by entraining other's brainwaves."

"Amazing!" Aissa was enamored with it all.

"Well, we've been looking for you, not just to bring you into the fold, but in your mind, in your memories, there may be a picture of an object that we've been searching for since your mother's death. A small leather-bound notebook. It is incredibly integral to the work of The Wave. If Marie can see it, she can gather the information inside it through a process similar to osmosis."

"Incredible," Aissa whispered with tears welling up in her eyes. "But I barely remember my mother, I don't think I will be able to help," she said shaking her head and wiping away her tears.

Marie then came and knelt in front of her and held her hands. As she did, a memory surrounded Aissa as if she were reliving it. She was in bed with her mother, in she and Asante's room. Stella was holding her and singing the, "Ready for the Day" song. All the words came easily out of her mouth as she began to sing along with her mother. *I am ready for the day, I am kind, I am brave. I'm exactly what I say, not tomorrow but today! I am ready for today, night is gone, I'm awake. There is no time anyway, let's have fun and create. Don't delay, ride the waves, I am ready for the day. I am ready for the day, I am ready for the day."*

Marie let go of her hand and her mother and the room disappeared. Overwhelmed with emotion, Aissa caused the ground beneath them to move. Aissa calmed herself and everyone and everything was still.

"Alrighty then," Obadias broke the silence. "Now that you see, you and Marie will spend a little time every day searching for your mother's notebook in your memories."

"What's in it, what's in the notebook?" Aissa asked.

"The knowledge that will give us the ultimate weapon against The Sephiren and free humanity from the guise of the veil," Obadias answered.

"Oh no pressure to find it then," Aissa smiled nervously.

Chapter 9
The Wave

Aissa and Marie were becoming the best of friends through their daily regression sessions. They were reliving the most joyful parts of Aissa's early childhood. Because Stella was in a perpetual state of hiding and moving, a lot of the memories they explored were of car rides where Aissa and Asante sat in the back seat of her Nissan Sentra playing games and taking in the majestic scenery, while Stella sang, told stories, and drove. Yet, they hadn't seen the ever-elusive black notebook, it had been six months.

The time did give Aissa the opportunity to dive into study with Obadias. They scoured some of the most ancient religious, political, and scientific texts of the world.

"So, you mean that the advent of Christ is contingent upon the awakening of man into The Now?" Aissa asked.

"Yes, the kingdom in which He speaks of returning for is alive in all of us, just hidden and disguised by the veil."

"And The Sephiren is working diligently to keep this truth as well as other realities hidden from man's visage."

"But why, in my training with The Sephiren, they deemed their motives to be in the pure interest of human civility?"

"Ultimately it comes down to control, if there were a true peaceful utopia on earth, the veil would be useless and The Sephiren would no longer have a purpose, without which they wouldn't exist. This new age where mankind will be elevated to his intended purpose aligned with Source will begin with The Aurora," Obadias and the others were convinced that either she or Asante was The Aurora spoken of. She wasn't sure what she believed at this point.

Besides falling deeper and deeper into the realm of true reality, Aissa also was falling deeply in love with Obadias. She wasn't sure of how he felt about her because he was genuinely open and sincere with everyone. She couldn't tell when she looked into his gorgeous eyes whether they were connecting with her soul the way she seemed to be connecting with his.

She was reflecting on all of this while mesmerized by the morning sunrise just beyond the garden on the cliff of the Palisades home when two strong hands grasped her shoulders from behind.

"Morning Girl Blue," *Obadias* She thought, breathing in his presence. He was referring to her favorite Stevie Wonder song that she had been playing in the house, morning, noon, and night for the past two days.

"Morning, Rasta!" She teased back as he was perpetually listening to Bob Marley on his headphones. He came around and sat next to her on the cliff.

"What you thinking about out here?"

"Oh, just stuff," she quietly answered.

"We will find the notebook and then we will find your sister and father."

"How do you know they are still alive?"

"The seer that led me to you, let me see both you and your sister but more than that, I have hope, and that same hope will guide you if you let it." He seemed to get shy at this moment.

"What is it?" Aissa waited with bated breath.

"You are the evidence of my hope for humanity and you are evidence of the hope for my heart."

Aissa stopped breathing for several moments.

"Heeyyyyy," shouted Marie as she approached. "Y'all ready for the day?" Aissa's heart screamed *not just yet*. Obadias got up as Marie sat down.

"Catch y'all later, I know you've got to get into it."

Aissa put her head down.

Marie finally caught on and on offered, "I'm pretty off for a telepath, huh? I ruined it, didn't I?"

Aissa shook her head and started to laugh.

Marie replied with "I just deferred it a bit, but it's coming."

"If you knew, how come you didn't say anything this whole time?"

"You ain't gonna use me for romancing the stone, you are going to have to do that all on your own," they laughed together.

*　　*　　*

Aissa could feel the night's cool ocean breeze through the car window, it woke her as the Nissan Sentra decelerated. They pulled into a dirt road as the car's headlights flashed over a wooden sign that read, "The Eslan Institute, By Reservation Only," in white. They drove up a hill with trees on one side and the ocean just beyond a cliff on the other. She looked over at her sister in the moonlight, she was still asleep. Aissa could feel the top of her head opening. A tingling and warmth grew from the energy source at the crown of her head and traveled throughout her entire body as they climbed higher and higher up the hill. They pulled in front a mansion made of glass and wood. Three men were waiting in front in white linen robes to the ground.

"Wake up girls, we've made it."

Asante began to stir. Aissa watched as Stella turned off the engine grabbed her purse and stepped out of the car. The three men walked toward her and embraced her. Her mother seemed to fall into the comfort and peace of their arms. She walked back to the car and opened the back seat door for Aissa and Asante to get out. Aissa stepped out onto the ground and a surge of energy entered her body through her bare feet.

"This is my youngest, Aissa," Stella introduced her as she stepped out of the car. The tallest of the three men stepped forward and bent down so he was nearly eye level with Aissa.

"My name is David, it is a pleasure to meet you," and opened his arms for her to hug him. She felt her body move toward him and a white light greeted her as she did.

Home. "Is this our new house, Mommy?" She turned and asked Stella, who was trying to coax Asante out of the car.

"Let the child sleep, I'll have Nyrraw and Brad watch over her." He motioned for the other two men standing next to him to come forward. "And we'll come back for her once I've shown you around and chatted a bit."

Stella reluctantly closed the door.

Inside the mansion, iron and copper fixtures hung from the very high ceilings. In the large sitting room, there were several people engaged in conversation dressed in white. They walked through the room past all of them and entered a library. Stella motioned for Aissa to sit at a large glass table with a beautiful marble stone as its base. The reflection of the fire from the fireplace danced across the glass in the dim light. While Aissa was transfixed by the refracted light in the table, she noticed she could also see David and her mother talking in the reflection of the glass as well.

Stella went into her large bag and pulled out the notebook. "Will you please look over my annotations and let's discuss your thoughts in the morning." David grabbed the notebook as the room disappeared into thin air.

Aissa opened her eyes and she was on the cliff back in Palisades. She turned to find Marie on the ground shaking, she looked like she was having a seizure.

"Obadias!" Aissa screamed out.

The next few moments felt like hours. Time seemed to slow as Obadias ran out of the house to them.

"What happened?"

"We found it! And when I came to she was on the ground like this! Do something!"

The others came running out of the house.

"Ride the Wave," Obadias said calmly as he sat down with his legs crossed in front of him. Everyone began to do the same. He placed Marie in his lap. He then put two fingers on each of her temples. Aissa watched as she sat down.

"Marie is having a 'kundalini' experience. She must have tried to glean what is in the notebook and the knowledge is too great for her at this moment, sending her into another dimension. She's lost right now. We need to help her ground and come back.

"Aissa, we are all aligning with the elements around us to create a safe way back to this dimension for Marie. I need you to align with the plates beneath us to complete the process."

Aissa immediately began to feel the connection between herself and the earth. She honed in on the plates and as she did a bubble of iridescent purple light surrounded the group. Marie's body began to slow. She began to breathe deeply and rhythmically. She opened her eyes, tears rolling down her face. A moment later the purple shield receded.

Marie cleared her throat and said, "We need them both. Michael, he is the door, and Asante is the key."

Chapter 10
The Truth

The blowing in Asante's ear began as a whisper as she stepped out of Obadias' vintage nineteen seventy-seven Cadillac El Dorado. The sun's mid-morning rays shone through the trees and lit the path to the cabin as the mist from the lake cooled the air. It created a spectacular array of light. The whispering in her ears grew into a rushing wind yet the air all around her was still. Multi-colored pebbled, gray stones adorned the path.

Each step Asante took, she felt lighter and lighter, almost as if she were leaving her body. As she took her first step up onto the stairs of the porch, the door opened. Tears began to pour down Asante's face. The eyes that met her, mirrored her own, yet with the most incredibly green hazel pigment dusted with gold. Aissa. She ran up the rest of the steps to embrace her sister. All of the pain, fear, and loss left her body as they hugged and kissed each other's faces, examined each other's' hair, hands, and skin. They began to Eskimo, butterfly, and sissy kiss within moments. It was as if they were never apart, not so much in words at first, both not knowing where to start. Then Aissa took the lead inviting Asante into the large living room.

A huge sectional was in the center of the room and large potted plants were everywhere. A water fountain made of stone took up most of one wall, while the opposite wall had a very large bay window with a view of the lake.

They sat on the couch, looked at each other and erupted into laughter. Once they collected themselves, Asante started with, "Obadias has given me an idea of what's going on, but who is after us, who has been manipulating our lives all this time and why?"

"It's not just our lives, sister, it's all of humanity. There is the reality that you experienced, which most of the population on earth knows. A reality filled with distractions, unfulfilling jobs, education without knowledge, false ideas that continue to separate man from himself and universe in order to negate what we are truly intended for."

"Which is?" Asante interjected.

"To live harmoniously connected with Source and all that we encounter," Aissa said simply.

Asante laughed out loud, "You mean utopia, paradise on earth? You don't really believe that's possible?" Asante declared more than asked.

"I know that I am your baby sister but if you will allow me to teach you, you will lead and teach us how to achieve that said paradise."

Asante couldn't help herself, she interrupted again, "But how do you know?"

"First, because Mommy knew and gave her life aiming to protect the knowledge. Second, because I've studied the most ancient and obscure texts on this planet and they all point to the same thing, a coming of a new age. And third, people I trust with the ability to see various paths into what is relatively known as the future have seen it. But trust me, sister, there's no easy road ahead and if you think that what you've experienced up until now was a tornado, buckle up because there never really was a Kansas to begin with."

Asante was doing her best to follow her sister down the rabbit hole, but the reality she had known only a few weeks earlier still filled her mind. Despite what she had encountered over the past few weeks, she struggled with letting go of the reality that had given her stability. However, she was determined to know the truth about the new actuality her sister described.

She answered with, "So who has been behind the design of these constructs that we interpret as life?"

Aissa smiled. "It's not so much as who has designed them," she asserted, "as much as it is, who are those that guarantee these constructs remain in place. That would be The Sephiren and other sub-factions working on their behalf. They have created a grid where most of the population doesn't veer off course. The grid's purpose is to monitor and maintain the status quo. Through means such as media, entertainment, false religion, politics, even the Patriot Act, all serve to keep us in place. We call this the veil. And most people do as society would have them do. They keep their heads down, go to work, watch the game, and go to some type of religious gathering. And in turn, they are mainly disconnected from their lives. They carry all the burden of the responsibility that life puts on them, yet they enjoy very little of the possibility that it also offers. They ultimately become slaves of these constructs. Never aware enough to actually be in The Now and enjoy the love and power that flows through it. And although society has changed or evolved per se, The Sephiren's aim hasn't. Enslave their hearts and minds, restrain their power.

"We are a part of the opposing force. Our mother and our mother's mother, going back several centuries were keepers of The Wave. We are the incarnation of this knowledge. Our name came out of the old Native Wappo myth of The Flood. But our name also refers to the waves that are described as force in chi, qui, chakras, and the Holy Spirit, if you will. All of them are pointing to the same thing and are found in the body in the form of frequency, thus The Wave. Our intention is to bring as much of the population into The Now or integration as possible so that the wave can be accessed, and man will enter into a new age. Our parents discerned the identity of The Aurora—or the one who would usher in this new age—freeing humankind of the veil and the grid from which we've been enslaved. Again, Mommy was killed for this knowledge."

"What does that mean?" Asante still wasn't clear about the picture Aissa was painting.

"Let me ask you something?" Aissa asked back. "How did you heal Seager?"

"Not this again, I don't know." Asante shook her head.

"We need to figure out how you were able to heal those blood vessels without any knowledge or training in integration or entrainment."

Aissa searched Asante's face. "I have no idea, the only thing I remember was an intense connection to my desire for him to successfully make it through the surgery and when Massah damaged the arteries, that desire outweighed the possibility of any other outcome. It was so much so that I was convinced she was mistaken and hadn't actually damaged them."

"So your connection to your intention forced your being into The Now. I can see that, but how did you heal those vessels without consciously entraining them?" She asked more to herself than Asante. Aissa's face was pensive as she pontificated the dilemma.

"There is one more thing." Asante offered. "It first happened during the surgery and has continued to happen since."

"What, what is it?" Aissa was on the edge of her seat.

"I know it's going to sound crazy but as I began to handle the arteries, again when Obadias rescued me, and yet again outside, just before we were reunited, I felt a distinct blowing in my ears," Asante recalled.

"What do u mean a blowing, like wind?"

"Yes, as if there is someone or something blowing air directly into my ears."

"I've never heard of anything like this but I'm sure it's the key to how you entrained the cells in those blood vessels."

"What does that mean?" Asante begged, still needing clarity.

"It means we need to get Michael sooner than later," Aissa exclaimed with excitement in her eyes.

"Michael who, our dad?"

"Yes!" Aissa's entire face lit up.

Asante didn't know how to process this information. Part of her heart was full of joy in the possibility of finally reuniting with her father but underneath that joy was resentment toward a dad that abandoned his family when they needed him the most.

"Where is he, I thought he was dead all this time?"

"No, my dear sister, he's very much alive being held in the psychiatric ward at Sing Sing Correctional Facility." Aissa disclosed.

"How do u know, why is he there?" Asante asked.

"Daddy was a very powerful telepath with the ability to not only entrain other's brainwaves but radio waves, electromagnetic waves, and so on. He essentially had the power to disrupt television transmissions, control and manipulate anyone, and The Sephiren couldn't stop him. They couldn't have him destroying their perfectly constructed grid, he could have just about brought an end to the guise over humanity all by himself."

"What did they do to him?" Asante almost whispered to herself.

"All we know is that The Sephiren lured him and Mommy into a trap of some sort, and Mommy escaped with you by her side and me in her belly.

"The Sephiren has held him captive for the past twenty-five years for crimes he obviously didn't commit. Ever since they killed Mommy to attain the knowledge she had written down in her notebook, they have been trying to manipulate him into decoding her writing. He and Mommy created a cipher to protect the contents of the notebook.

"Our telepath Marie has been able to connect to him, though, their communication has been sporadic at best. All the experiments and brainwashing they've done on him has taken a toll on his sense of self and his overall wellness. At this point, he believes Marie is a figment of his imagination. She believes he will soon break and The Sephiren will have the knowledge to stop The Aurora from ushering in the new age or 'utopia' as you called it. We have to rescue him before that happens."

"So how do we get him?"

"Well, we have a plan but it's not going to make much sense to you until you meet some people."

"Well, where are they, because I was going to say this is a mighty big cabin for just you and Obadias. Is this some type of Wave Headquarters?"

"That's exactly what it is my love, exactly."

At this, she grabbed Asante's hand and guided her through the kitchen, past what appeared to be a music room, to a large atrium in the center of the house. It was like walking into a jungle. Birds were singing, little monkeys swung from branches, and water was flowing somewhere because Asante could smell and hear it. They made it to the center of the room, where there was a descending staircase.

Aissa turned to Asante and said, "I asked everyone to stay down here while we had a moment to reconnect."

She motioned for Asante to follow her. At the bottom of the staircase, there appeared to be titanium door, next to it, was a thumbprint keypad, as well as retina scan. Aissa went through the process to open the door. The powerful metal slid from left to right. They stepped into an LED-lit corridor, walked a few paces, and stepped into what looked like a war room. Asante stopped in her tracks, the first face she saw was that of her resident Massah David.

Chapter 11
The Sephiren

Brennan stepped out of his black nineteen fifty-eight Chevy Impala. He loved driving her down the coast to LA. He and Asante had taken the trip many times to catch a concert or spend time in Malibu. This time he was still here for Asante though she was still off-grid. Dr. Schmidt would assist in locating her with her quantum computer. The mirrored glass building on Sunset Boulevard said Quanta in silver outlined in teal as he walked through the entrance's sliding doors. He nodded to security and headed straight for the elevator. Once inside he took out a keycard that accessed a retina scan. After he was scanned, a green light illuminated indicating he was to go to the top floor. However, when the elevator began to move it descended. After waiting ten to fifteen seconds, he had reached his desired floor, some fifty feet below sea level, the Southern California Sub-Faction of The Sephiren, Quanta.

The large room had rows and rows of desks with people and computers all working to maintain the veil on their section of the grid. Beyond the open workspace was a staircase to a conference room that overlooked the bullpen of workers. He headed for the stairs, as he did, Ethan Vanderneiss approached after he came out of the men's room.

"Valdis," he muttered.

"Vanderneiss" Brennan retorted.

"Lost your girlfriend, huh?" Brennan ignored him. Ethan continued. "Ya know, if she is The Aurora, The Sephiren will never allow you to be together, so you might as well get that pitiful look out of your eyes now before you're removed from the Council." He started to laugh as Brennan left him at the bottom of the stairs and began to ascend to the office above.

Brennan was upset because he knew that Vanderneiss spoke the truth. His plan was to find Asante and persuade her to become a part of The Sephiren but if she is The Aurora their relationship was over. The Sephiren would never allow it. His sense of duty and his heart were at war. But first things first; get her back.

He knocked on the door. Adele Vanderneiss answered.

"Hello, Darling," she stretched out the words in her fabricated accent.

"Hello, Adele," he mustered dryly.

He walked passed her directly to Dr. Schmidt.

Adele, excusing herself, said, "Well, I'll leave you to it." She left the room and closed the door behind her.

Elouise Schmidt looked over her spectacles up at Brennan as she sat typing on her computer at her oversized mahogany desk. Her vintage garb and desk were such an odd contrast to the modern and almost futuristic setting of Quanta.

"I suspect, by your presence here, that your level three priority yielded no results?" She asked more rhetorically than anything else.

"That's correct. The APB produced nothing. The Vanderneiss' satellites produced nothing, traffic and security cameras nothing. Farraday and Fairchild have sent me to avoid making this a national security measure," Brennan lied. He hadn't reported back to Farraday and Fairchild yet, he was attempting to locate Asante before they did.

Brennan continued, "Although we both know that even if we do, Sephiren doesn't have a device that will locate her as efficiently as your quantum computer."

"No, they don't." Schmidt's thin lips barely moved in response. "By the time they pull their heads out of their asses, my computer will have disregarded all moot possibilities and delivered the true location of your love. Isn't that why you are really here, Brennan? To save your love?"

"Yes," he gave up, not knowing if she was onto his lie or just reading his emotions.

"I will help you, but what are you willing to give me in return?"

"What do you want, I thought we were all on the same side here, fighting for humanity?"

"Yes, blah, blah, blah. I want Stella's notebook."

Brennan was genuinely confused. "The Council has had that notebook locked away behind some high-security vault for twenty-five years now." *What wasn't she saying, what had she found out?*

"Let's just say I know there's another copy of it and your girlfriend very likely has it."

Quantum Computer, she already knows Asante's location. He surmised.

"Ok, I will get the notebook for you, but what do you want it for?"

"That's not any of your concern, just go get your girlfriend, she's in the Mayacamas Mountains, ten miles outside of Calistoga."

"Dr. Farraday, line two," the intercom echoed as Emily Farraday looked out of her office window onto the fog rolling in onto the bay.

"It's me." Fairchild declared.

"I know," Farraday replied with impatience. "What is it?"

"Brennan's ocular camera just downloaded footage of him visiting Schmidt."

"And? Did she give up the location of Asante or not?"

"She did. She also alluded to Asante being in possession of a copy of Stella's notebook. Which more than likely means she's with Aissa. We have a team that should intercept before Valdis gets there.

"Geothermal imaging from the drone of the location in the Mayacamas Mountain range show at least fifteen people inside the compound and another ten canvassing the surrounding area. This is most likely the base for The Wave. Are we taking them all out or just recovering zero-one-four-three?"

"Recover zero-one-four-three, Aissa, and copy of the notebook. Eliminate the rest. It's about time we got rid of this nuisance of a faction and set the scales back in real balance."

*   *   *

Massah's eyes again filled with water as she ran up to Asante and embraced her. Asante was overwhelmed with emotion.

"Once we located you, we had to have someone close to you that wouldn't raise any suspicion." Obadias recounted, "We sent Massah because she's in the process of learning how to integrate and entrain. We knew she could shadow you, yet her knowledge is limited, so in case she was caught she couldn't give up any information. We only brought her here to headquarters for the first time after you were taken from Fairchild's estate."

"I'm so happy you are okay!" Massah exclaimed when an alarm started to ring out and flashing lights lit up the room they were in.

"What's going on?" Asante asked.

Aissa and an olive-skinned, bald man rushed past them and looked at a monitor. It seemed like some type of security system. On the screen, an eagle appeared. *Why is an alarm going off for an eagle?* Asante wondered. But as she did, Aissa pressed a key and the imaging on the monitor changed into an x-ray of sorts. Now the flying eagle's insides were apparent and it was obvious that it wasn't a bird at all but some type of drone.

"They found us. Evacuate now!" She flipped open another box on the same desk and inside was an iridescent blue button. She pressed it and the door which they had entered closed shut. All the screens of the computers and monitors in the room began to run code. The walls moved and exposed guns and weaponry which every person in the room began to pack onto their bodies. Pre-packed backpacks were now being put on by everyone in the room.

The olive-skinned man turned to Asante and her heart stopped. His eyes. Hazel large eyes met her own, as he grabbed her hand, a charge of electricity shot through her body. She felt like she was levitating.

"Asante," he stated her name, grounding her.

"Yes," she whispered.

"Take this," he handed her a gun and began to put a backpack over her shoulders.

"But I don't know how to use this," she admitted.

"You will," and then he was gone into the rush of people moving about.

Aissa's voice grabbed her attention. "Abort minus two minutes." Aissa grabbed what looked like a flash drive and took Asante's free hand. "Follow me, we're going to get out of here." She then opened another door using retina and fingerprint security. Inside was a dimly lit tunnel. "We have built miles of intertwining tunnels to get out of here off-grid. We will rendezvous in three days at the Eslan Institute. They are friends of The Wave."

Just then Obadias, Massah, and Marie were at their side. They began to run into the tunnels.

Chapter 12
Chelo

The air from the Pacific Coast Highway wafted into the van while Aissa and Obadias engaged in heavy conversation in the front seats. Asante woke as their voices rose.

"If she doesn't have some other type of tracker that you missed, how did they find us at the compound?" Aissa asked.

"I can't figure that part out, but we'll have Chelo take a look at her when we get to Eslan," Obadias replied.

"If they are not already waiting for us when we get there." Aissa snapped.

"What would you have us do, Aissa, we can't just leave her!" Obadias shot back.

"I'm not saying that I just wish we knew more..."

"We're awake back here!" The blonde, caramel-skinned girl sitting next to Asante, broke up the conversation. She turned to Asante and introduced herself, "I am Marie, I am a telepath of sorts and I'm happy to finally meet you!" She was warm and very bubbly considering the situation they were obviously in.

Asante shook her head and uttered. "It's a pleasure, are you the one communicating with my father?"

"Yup, that'd be me. As well as self-appointed referee between those two!" Pointing to Aissa and Obadias.

"Are they together?" Asante mouthed.

"Very much so, too much so at times." Marie smiled.

"We are here," Obadias announced. They pulled off Pacific Coast Highway and ascended a hill with ocean on one side and forest on the other. Then Asante saw the sign of the Eslan Institute and she immediately felt at peace as if she were coming home.

"We spent a good part of our early childhood here before mama settled us in Oakland when you started school." Aissa offered.

The beautiful wood and glass mansion they were approaching was vaguely familiar to Asante. As their van stopped, the front door opened, and a man with white linen robes, mocha clear skin, white hair and beard to match came out of the house to greet them. Aissa barely waited for the engine to stop before she hopped out of the van and ran into the man's arms.

Asante said to herself, "Nyrraw."

Marie overheard her and said, "You do remember, then?"

"I don't know that I remember, per se, but I know that man's name is Nyrraw." They all got out of the van.

"Asante," Nyrraw breathed in as he hugged her. She could feel her entire being become present in his embrace. She opened her eyes and all that she encountered in the morning's light was more vivid and vibrant. The flowers' colors shined and sparkled like gems. The air was fresh and cool, she took in a clearing breath and looked into his eyes.

"You are the key, now we need to find the door, so that we all may walk through."

Asante smiled but was still so unsure. *How can I be the key, so much of my life was entrenched in the veil?* She wasn't sure of what was actually reality. She felt like her whole life had been a fabrication of The Sephiren and she was a mere puppet in their play.

Almost as though Nyrraw read her thoughts he said, "There's so much more of you to know, you will find your highest self and we will be the reflection of Source which flows through you." He smiled warmly and motioned for them to follow him into the house.

"The others arrived last night, only Chelo is awake, I think finishing his morning meditations on the cliffs below."

After a tour, they congregated in the open kitchen. All of The Wave's members were present and introductions and happy reunions were made. Nyrraw ran this sub-faction of The Wave as his father, David, had done so before him. Asante vaguely remembered him caring for her as a child. But she couldn't believe that J.StaRR was his sister and that she and The Misfitz were a part of The Wave. She had heard their music on the radio and seen them on award shows, but to find out they were a part of this faction and were actively countering the efforts of The Sephiren was mind-blowing.

Marie with her ability to locate and communicate with people, glean an understanding of objects through osmosis and see possible futures was amazing.

She also met Brad who she instinctively felt like they would be working closely together but didn't know why. He had blown her mind with his ability to seemingly disappear into thin air. Which apparently had to do with his skill to manipulate what others see than him actually not being there. However, his intelligence and understanding of how things work were his shining attributes.

Then she saw *him* enter the house from the large glass doors overlooking the ocean. It was the same olive-skinned man from the compound. His lean chiseled frame only adorned swim trunks as he walked in, looking aloof at best.

"Chelo, come, have you met Asante?" Nyrraw asked as he motioned for him to come into the kitchen with the rest of the group. Asante could feel the room fading from her peripheral. Chelo walked up to her and her knees buckled a bit beneath her.

"Good to officially meet you, Asante." His words seemed affectionate to her. She felt drawn to him, her feelings were inexplicable as she couldn't find any appropriate words or phrases in response.

"Cat got your tongue?" Aissa interjected. Asante's face flushed with deep rouge.

"Nice to meet you." She finally managed.

"Now that you have returned. We need to figure out how The Sephiren found us. Can you scan Asante to see if we missed anything?" Aissa asked.

"Sure," Chelo answered as he came closer to Asante. She felt as though she might faint.

"What are you going to scan, how?" Asante asked.

"Don't worry it won't hurt, I can entrain and source all electromagnetic waves. If there's a device hidden in your body I will be able to differentiate between it and your body's natural frequencies."

His eyes began to look over every inch of her body. Though fully clothed she felt as though she was as naked as a newborn babe.

"Nothing," he offered once he had completely taken in her being a moment later.

"That's impossible, what are we not seeing?" Aissa was visibly bothered.

"We don't know what we don't know. But what's important is that we now have Asante, we can get your father and unlock the door. Let's not forget our intentions here, Aissa." Nyrraw maintained.

"Believe me, I am not, but what if we are literally walking into a trap? What will happen to all of our intended plans, to our parents' sacrifices? What will it all have meant? More importantly what will happen to humankind if The Sephiren and the other sub-factions have free rein and are unchecked, what hope will any of us have?"

They all began to speak at once and argue. Asante felt more confused and more unsure than ever. Chelo grabbed her hand and they slowly stepped backward away from the group and out of the kitchen. He led her across the living area and out of the doors from which he had entered.

The ocean's morning air greeted them and immediately calmed Asante. Chelo led her down a dirt path to several cliffs. They reached the highest one where a small clearing of grass had a tree trunk as its center. He motioned for her to sit on it next to him.

"It's all a bit much isn't it?"

Asante didn't know what to say. Overwrought with emotion, tears filled her eyes and began to stream down her face which she buried in her crossed arms.

"Close your eyes," Chelo whispered and kneeled in front of her. She lifted her head to meet his gaze. Asante did as he said and as he held her hands in his she was greeted by a warm blanket of darkness. A moment later the blowing in her ears began. As it turned into a rushing wind, lights that resembled stars began to appear. The stars began to move through the darkness turning into streaks of light pushing her body forward. Then a bright white light surrounded her. In it, she began to see images of her and Chelo in various settings and clothing.

T.O.R.N.

In one vision they held each other and kissed in the moonlight on a black beach. In another, they washed each other in a bathtub, laughing and playing with bubbles. In yet another, they held a child cooing and smiling. In each of the visions, they were seemingly in different lifetimes. Then she saw them hovering above the earth from space. He looked into her eyes as the blue hue from the earth's reflection glowed in his countenance and smiled, "We've always been and will always be." She opened her eyes back on the cliff to find him still smiling at her. Her past, and all that The Sephiren had done, now seemed like a faraway dream. She was ready to let go and enter into The Now because although she didn't know how she would rise to all that was being asked of her, she did know that love waited for her here and now, and with that, all things are possible.

Chapter 13
Michael

On one of the more secluded beaches in Pismo Beach, California, Michael rubbed lotion on Stella's back as she leaned forward into her butterfly stretch. She inhaled deeply as he massaged her achy muscles. Eight months pregnant, she needed every bit of this attention to her body. She exhaled releasing the tension.

Stella opened her eyes to see Asante running toward the incoming tide and yelled, "Not too far Asante, wait for Mommy!"

"You better go grab her before the ocean does." Michael joked.

Stella took one more deep breath and stood in one motion. She began to run toward her daughter, as she did, she saw Asante standing at the water's edge and a wave the size of a tsunami rolled toward her in the distance. The faster Stella ran to Asante, the further Asante and the shoreline became, yet the wave got closer and closer. The sky became darker and more ominous with each passing moment. Just as the tsunami seemed as though it would swallow up her precious child, Asante turned around to face the wave, held up her hands in the direction of the oncoming doom and the water stood still.

Stella, finally able to reach Asante, wrapped her arms around her daughter's small frame. The wave disappeared and the sun was shining brightly as it was a moment before. Stella looked around the desolate beach and all was tranquil. Michael waved to them and smiled from their blanket. She picked up Asante who seemed to be unaware of what she had just seen and began walking back toward him. *Was it some type of vision?* She had been having dreams that felt more like nightmares and although she would wake up frightened, Stella could never remember the details of her nightly terrors.

As she got closer Michael could read her face and he ran to her. "What's wrong, what happened?"

"I saw something but I'm not sure what it was? There was a tsunami coming in from the ocean, headed straight for us when I tried to get to Asante, I couldn't! And just when I thought all was lost, Asante turned toward the wave and was able to control it somehow," Stella was still obviously shaken.

"What do you think it means?" Michael asked with deep concern in his eyes. Stella looked up to meet his gaze as the setting sun's light danced in the flecks of gold in his green eyes, she didn't want to burden him today, they rarely were able to have days like this, days without the imminent threat of The Sephiren invading their reality. She didn't know what she saw but all was well now, that's all she needed.

"I'll meditate on it later and see if I can glean some discernment about what it means, in the meantime, Mama's hungry, what did u pack in that basket?"

Michael pulled she and Asante close to him, he whispered into her short hair, kissing her as he did, "I love you, but this burden is not yours alone to bear, no matter how powerful you are," he pulled back, smiling and took in the vision of his beautiful family. "Let's eat," he continued as he grabbed each of their hands and led them back to the blanket.

At dusk, they finished their meal and began to pack up. Michael stood up to get one good body stretch before they loaded up and got back in their nineteen sixty-seven VW Westfalia Camper Van. They had one hundred or so miles to cover before they could find a safe place for them to sleep. As he reached for the sky, it was as if he had been struck in the head with an unseen object. He fell to the ground holding both sides of his head.

"Daddy!" Asante cried out as Stella rushed to his side and held his head in her hands. He opened his eyes after a few moments and said, "They have Emily!"

"You know it's a trap when's the last time that you even heard from her?"

"Since before Asante was born but what does that matter, Stella?"

She looked at him intently, then, "Michael, is it possible she's working with The Sephiren? What if they turned her, you know how power hungry she's always been?"

"Again Stella, what does it matter, she's my sister?" He got up and started searching for something in his backpack.

"What are you looking for? Listen to me!"

He found what he was after. He pulled out a map and pencil and wrote coordinates at the top of it. After a moment of locating the proper longitudinal and latitudinal points, he drew a circle.

"This is where they are holding her, it's in San Francisco," he looked up at Stella with determination written all over his face.

"Wait, how do you know?"

"Because in my vision she was holding a sign that had these coordinates and twenty-two hundred on it, while a gun was pointed at her head."

"Then you know it's a trap! Michael, what will happen to us if something happens to you?" Stella pleaded.

"I can't leave my sister to die. I will be a shadow of who I am if I do. And what will happen to us if we go down that path? We are no better than the forces we are up against. They don't value human life past the control they exert over it. I will not succumb to that control!"

She knew it was useless but she also knew that she couldn't allow him to go alone.

Reading her, he simply answered, "No, I will not have it. I will drop you guys off here in Benicia," he pointed to a location outside of San Francisco. "You'll wait three hours for me. If I can't communicate with you or show up in person, you get out of there, you hear me, Stella?" There was no point in fighting him now, she cleared her mind and began to pack up the rest of their belongings.

As they drove up the highway 101 toward Northern California, Stella felt helpless. Her anger at Michael was building as was the feeling that this might be the last time they may ever see him alive. Her higher-self won the internal battle and she decided to make the best of an impossible situation.

"Aissa," she offered, cutting the silence of the past seventy-five miles.

"Excuse me?" Michael asked cautiously.

"That will be her name, it also means grateful like Asante's name."

"Is it a girl's name this time?" He asked with a smirk. They laughed as they both had thought Asante was a boy before she was born and decided to keep the name once she surprised them, though it was traditionally an African male name.

"Yes but if we're wrong this time? Aissa won't work for a little boy." At this, they smiled nervously at each other and held hands. There was so much to say, but everything felt false to Stella so she decided to be still and take in the love emanating from Michael. This time he broke the silence as they approached the city limits.

"You have the notebook, make sure to use the cipher we created to encode it once you can safely get to David at Eslan, but stay off-grid for a while before attempting to reach him. If what we've interpreted about The Aurora is true, you, Asante and little Aissa will be in danger, you must be strong..." He stopped, taking in the despair in her countenance. She began to cry and rub her belly. He pulled over. He turned to check on Asante, who was sleeping soundly in the back.

"You are talking as if we won't be together, do you know how unnerving that is, coming from you?" She wailed.

"There's nothing I can do about the position that I am in. But you do not share the same fate. So, now I need you to do something about the position you are in. The fate of humanity could rest in the hands of one of our girls, they need you."

"They need us both, Michael!" She shot back in anger, feeling alone and abandoned, more than inspired. He had nothing more. They rode the rest of the way in silence. After another hour or so they pulled into a small motel. Michael got out without saying another word and went to check them in. He returned a few moments later.

"You're in room eight, here's the key. I'm going to get out here and walk two miles down the road to the gas station and call a cab. Stella, I love you and my girls with all that I am. Ride the wave baby girl, until I see you again!" He leaned in and kissed her from the depths of his soul. But before she opened her eyes from their embrace, he had shut the door and was walking away into the night's shadows.

*   *   *

The cab pulled up to the street sign that read Maple Street. He handed the driver thirty-five bucks and stepped out into the moist night air. He checked his watch as the cab drove away, 21:45. What he hadn't explicitly spelled out for Stella was his suspicion that The Sephiren vaguely or precisely knew where they were in Pismo Beach. The amount of time designated on the sign was almost the exact amount of time it took him to get here, happenstance, he thought not. He wasn't willing to risk all of them being taken, if it was his family they wanted, they'd have to deal with him first.

As he approached the huge Georgian estate, he caused all the street lamps and lights of the adjacent homes to go out. He stood squarely in the cul-de-sac driveway and caused the ground lights and all the lights in the huge estate to go out at once. A moment later the front doors opened and Emily's short shiny blonde hair sparkled in the moonlight. She took several steps closer to her brother. Electric currents like mini lightning bolts illuminated in her hands, her eyes wild in the reflection of the blue hue coming from their currents.

Michael shouted, "Emily, what have you done?"

"Oh, dear brother, you can't hide them from us any longer!"

With this, she shot a burst of electricity directly into his chest, just fast and strong enough to catch him off guard and knock him unconscious. She stood over his body as men came out of the house to where they were.

"Hurry up, he'll only be out for a moment or two!" she yelled. They lifted up his limp body. "Administer the cocktail immediately, Carmichael," she dismissively said to one of the men.

He nodded and answered, "Yes, Dr. Farraday."

*   *   *

Stella sat straight up in the bed in a cold sweat. She looked over at the clock on the nightstand, it read 12:12 am. They had him, she could no longer feel her connection to him. But what she could feel with every part of herself was "Run."

T.O.R.N.

They had slept in their clothes, so she picked up a sleeping Asante, grabbed her keys and bag, and a moment later was back on the 101, determined to protect her girls.

Chapter 14
The Exchange

Tiki torches lit the path to the third and largest cliff at the Eslan Institute. On a clearing, more torches lit the ocean night air in a circle of twelve lights. Asante looked around the circle. The faces new and old greeted her gaze with a warmth that was somehow familiar. She was home. However, she also felt a sense of expectation in each one's visage. *Do they think I am The Aurora?* Although no one expressed this possibility explicitly to her, she could sense it in how they looked at her. It didn't matter now, what was in front of her was getting her father out of Sing Sing.

Marie had explained that the best weapon they had in freeing Michael was Michael himself. They needed to create a path from the delusion The Sephiren had him believing back to The Now. Where he would be able to access who he is and walk himself out of Sing Sing. He apparently was that powerful while integrated. She was still murky on how this was going to work, but she was as ready as she was ever going to be as Nyrraw began to speak.

"Marie has told us that Michael believes Asante and Aissa are dead. The Sephiren has manipulated his mind into believing that he is responsible for their deaths. He is lost in his own guilt of abandoning them which is fueling the lie that they have constructed. Marie will create a connection to him through his dream state and when his consciousness links with her own, she will travel here with him via the astral plane. He will only be present and visible for a moment or two max."

What is an astral plane? Asante wondered.

"It's a dimension without physical form. Where our consciousness or soul experiences itself amongst the formless. I found an entrance or portal to it within my mind while I dreamt one night. I can access it and travel there while I'm integrated in order to locate and communicate with anyone still in form via their consciousness while they are dreaming." Marie expounded. "You are literally a dream-walker."

Asante couldn't believe it.

"Asante, you'll have to be integrated in order to guarantee that he sees you. Do your best to stay out of your head and into what you are experiencing now." Nyrraw interjected.

"Got it, now," Asante responded confidently though it was the furthest thing from what she felt.

Marie stepped away from the light of a tiki torch and into the center of the circle. She bent down and sat with her legs crossed and her hands on each knee, with her pointer finger and thumb touching in the direction of the sky. Everyone in the circle followed suit, as did Asante, though she didn't know what she was doing.

She instinctively closed her eyes and as she did, the rushing of wind started to blow in her ears. Then in her mind's eye, she saw Marie tapping the back of her father's shoulder in a space that was full of dancing light.

When he turned around he was annoyed to see her and started to brush her off, "I told you, woman, you need to prove that you are real if my daughters aren't dead, where are they?" Michael said turning his back to Marie once more.

"Michael, I have them, I just need you to come with me," something Marie had never been able to offer in the past without Asante's presence.

Back in the circle, Aissa got up, walked to Marie and sat down in front of her while she held her hands.

"Can you feel Aissa, she is sitting with me where I am at Eslan?" Marie asked Michael.

"How do I know it's her? Where's Asante?" Michael scoffed.

"Please travel back with me through the astral plane to Eslan and I promise she'll be there."

Michael turned back around in the swirling light toward Marie. Asante saw the pain in her father's face, he was so old and despondent, not how she remembered him at all. He reluctantly took Marie's hands. Asante opened her eyes and in the middle of the circle sat Marie and Aissa holding hands. Everyone else was still seated around the circle with their eyes closed but nothing else.

Then, a speck of light appeared above Aissa and Marie's heads. As she looked into the light it grew brighter and larger. At first, the light appeared to have shadows in it, but as she looked closer, the silhouette of a man became more visible. As she breathed in with the air that was now consistently blowing in her ears, she could see him more and more clearly with each breath. After about ten seconds she rose and walked to the center of the circle. Asante reached out her hand. Michael took in the sight of her and reached out to touch Asante's outstretched hand. As her finger touched the light of what was his finger, a stream of shared memories flooded her consciousness.

"Daddy," she whispered with tears in her eyes. He smiled down at her and then he was gone. The light disappeared and Aissa and Marie were looking at her.

*　　*　　*

Michael opened his eyes. *They are alive!* He let the weight of what he just learned wash over his body. He knew what he must do. However, he didn't know if he was capable of accomplishing it. He had not connected to himself much less any other element in twenty-five years. But they were alive and so was he, which meant they needed him. He started with this truth and began to fill his mind with what he could remember.

Stella, he had loved her with all his heart, she was his true north. Yet, he was not able to save her. He had tried to communicate with her when he could gather enough focus through the cocktail of drugs they were using to manipulate him. But The Sephiren had figured out a way to track his telepathic messages to her and used the information to pinpoint her location. He blamed himself for her death. The Sephiren compounded his guilt with the lie that his daughters were killed as well. All of it a manipulation that had cost him his life. But no more.

He thought of his family. First of his love for Stella enveloped his being. Next, he filled his mind of his hope for Asante and Aissa. Finally, he took three clearing breaths releasing all of it and entered into *The Now.* As he did, he could feel his energy centers begin to release and clear. He was healing. Then as electricity informs a light bulb so did the wave inform his body. Moments later he could feel the energy of the inmates in the cells next to him. He engaged with every detail of his prison. The electric currents that coursed through the cell doors connected to his body. It was now or never.

He moved toward the door of bars that held him. It was the middle of the night and the constraints on his mind gripped him with fear for a moment disrupting his connection to the present. In response, he allowed the knowledge of his children's lives into the moment and let go. The door to his cell opened. He walked down the corridor to the stairs. He descended the steps until he was on the first floor of the block.

A guard came through a set of double doors that were operated by another guard outside of the block to do his rounds. After the guard's initial surprise, he reached for his radio with one hand and gripped his baton with the other. Michael needed to act fast. He disrupted the radio's ability to transmit. The guard looked at the piece of equipment in his hand in a moment of disbelief, then looked into Michael's eyes. As they stared at each other, Michael began to entrain the guard's thoughts, then as if in a trance he asked Michael, "How can I help you?"

"Cuff me, and then lead me back through the block doors, explain to the other guard, that you found me in a pool of my own vomit and you are taking me to the medical ward." The guard did as he was instructed. A few moments later, Michael was escorted by the guard to the medical facility in the prison.

There were four medical staff on call as they walked in. Two were sitting at computers, while the other two were checking the inventory of medication. They all turned with looks of confusion and surprise as Michael and the prison guard entered. The supervisor stepped forward immediately determined to get to the bottom of what was going on.

"It's the middle of the night, what's the emergency? This inmate looks fine to me."

The guard began to run his story, but the supervisor wasn't going for it. Michael knew he had moments at best but was having trouble connecting telepathically to everyone in the room utilizing one frequency. Doubt was entering in his consciousness disrupting his connection to The Now once again. But this time fear began to envelop his consciousness.

* * *

"What's happening?" Asante asked Aissa and Marie.

"He saw you and he is remembering who he is, but I don't know if he's strong enough to get out of there on his own," Marie responded.

Nyrraw asked, "Marie, what do you see?" Marie closed her eyes and moments later whispered, "he's in trouble, he's doubting himself, thus cut off from his true power."

"Can we help him, what can we do?" Asante asked.

But no one seemed to have an answer. Aissa stood up and looked Asante in the eyes and said, "If anyone can do anything at this moment, it's you. Trust yourself and follow your instincts."

Asante had no clue, she was panicked, but she wouldn't lose him again. She looked down at Marie who was still sitting with her legs crossed in the center of the circle. Asante sat down in front of her and grabbed her hands. As she did, she could see her father in a room with a guard and four people that looked like nurses. She heard the words come out of her mouth before she could think about what she was doing.

"Daddy, can you hear me?"

"Asante," Michael responded.

"Ride the wave, Daddy, ride the wave."

Tears started to flood down his face. Asante then took a deep breath with as much air that could fill her lungs and blew out. As she did, Michael could feel the air fill his body as if she had given him a push back into reality and out of his fear. He opened his eyes to see everyone in the room staring up at him in awe. He was levitating, to his own surprise, he smiled at the power that his body was wielding at this moment, the power, Asante reminded him, was accessible at any moment.

He returned to the ground and said to the guard, "Unlock these cuffs." Again the guard did as he was instructed. Michael then turned to the three other staff members and said, "Return to your duties." As if in a trance, they all busied themselves with work. Finally to the supervisor, who patiently waited for his instructions, "Set up an ambulatory transport now." Ten minutes later Michael was in the back of an ambulance riding south toward New York City. He knew he had to get off-grid immediately, but more than that his mind was reeling with possibility because he now knew Asante was in fact, The Aurora.

Chapter 15
The Plot

It had been a week in a half since Michael had escaped Sing Sing. However, no one from The Wave had heard from him and Marie hadn't been able to connect with him on a telepathic level. Aissa wasn't sure if he had escaped at all. Her doubt and anxiety built daily. Nyrraw had suggested that Michael was purposefully quiet and undetectable to negate any effort by The Sephiren to recapture him. But the silence was getting under all of their skin and The Sephiren was unusually silent as well. There was no APB out for Michael nor mention of his escape on any local or national television networks, which was odd according to Obadias and Aissa because The Sephiren notoriously used law enforcement to detain individuals that were a threat to the veil.

Asante and Chelo were tasked with the continued search of all social media and television networks for anything related to Michael. This morning all of the stations were abuzz with the new presidential candidate that replaced a senator who had to step down because of an infidelity scandal. Asante was about to change the channel when the new candidate came from behind a curtain and stepped up to the podium.

Her pulse started to race and sweat formed on her forehead as Chelo and the room disappeared from her view. Although he had traded his scruffy brown suit for a black one, there was no denying it. The presidential candidate was Mr. Douglas from the police station all those many years ago.

"What's wrong, Asante?"

Asante tried to speak, but she was having some type of post-traumatic episode. "It's, it's, it's...But, it's?"

"It's what, Asante?" Chelo urged her to answer. Asante continued to try, but nothing intelligible would come out of her mouth. "Aissa!" Chelo screamed out. A moment later, Aissa ran into the media room where she found Asante with a look of fear and confusion on her face and Chelo who wiped her brow.

"What is it, what's going on?" Aissa asked. Asante still too overwhelmed to speak, pointed at the television. Aissa stood still in her tracks. *Douglas*. A moment later.

"There they are. They are making their move." Chelo looked to Aissa for answers.

"It's The Sephiren. They are taking up a new strategy, more control, more visibility," Aissa concluded. Then she knelt down to face her sister. "Asante, breathe deeply. We knew The Sephiren would seek to deepen their dominance over the population. More and more individuals are no longer accepting their reality. That combined with you, me, and Daddy in the wind, they are operating out of fear which means they will ultimately meet their demise. Let's not forget, they are afraid of you, the possibility of you being The Aurora is why you were monitored all this time, you can bring an end to their existence. I know it's upsetting to see him, but we must move forward with our purpose." This calmed Asante a bit, but she was still anxious about her role in "our" purpose.

"So do you think I am The Aurora?"

"I think it's a very real possibility"

Asante decided to call out the elephant in the room. "We don't know if our father is alive or dead. And although Marie has transcribed the contents of Mommy's notebook, without him we are just as lost as we were before!" She nearly yelled at Aissa.

"Please have hope, we have you, Asante!" Aissa rebutted. Asante could feel a lump in her throat rise as she thought of her response.

"Who am I? I accidentally performed a miracle? I don't know how I'm doing any of this. I can barely wrap my mind around the possibility of what you all can do yet I've seen it with my own eyes." She shook her head as she looked at the floor.

Chelo then stepped forward and interjected. "You will learn. Be patient with yourself. We will help you see for yourself what we hope for you and all of humanity. Living in The Now, being in The Now, no longer chained by the pains of your past, nor the anxieties of your future."

"You make it sound so easy." She sniffled and continued to look at the ground.

"It's not easy, but it is as natural as breathing, and when you truly find your still breath you will find The Now and all that flows through it." He touched her chin gently and lifted Asante's head so that their eyes could meet. She smiled at him and all was well for the moment.

"So, when do we start?" Asante asked.

"We start now," Aissa and Chelo said in unison. "There's no time but The Now."

*   *   *

Brennan looked around the opulent sitting room as he had done many times before. However, today he was uneasy in a way that was new to him. Today he couldn't shake the memory of Asante as she was subdued by Carmichael, the guards, and himself not ten feet from where he now sat. He also had newly found misgivings about Farraday and Fairchild. It was as if he were a pawn in a larger battle for Asante. But, he hadn't seen his role until it was too late.

When he had reached the Mayacamas Mountains, the only people he found at The Wave headquarters were a part of The Sephiren. They had been there for at least two hours scouring it for clues as to how The Wave knew they were coming and where they might be headed. Which now Brennan was turning over in his mind, *how had The Sephiren found out their location?* He knew that Schmidt, because of her own interests in getting her hands on the notebook, hadn't given them up. This only left him. Which means Farraday and Fairchild had been monitoring him without his knowledge.

Today they had called him here to Maple Street to give him his new orders. But he was no one's puppet and he was determined to not be played again. Fairchild and Farraday entered the room and disrupted his train of thought.

"Oh, silly, silly Brennan, did you think you could have Asante all to yourself? Run off into paradise, or some cliché shit like that?" Fairchild started. Farraday smirked to herself and searched Brennan's face for a response. Brennan determined to not give anything up at this point, starred coldly back.

"The real question at this juncture is should you be trusted or discarded?"

79

Brennan opened his mouth to speak and Fairchild grasped at the air in a motion as if he were catching a bug. Brennan found his vocal cords had been affected by Fairchild's action.

"It was a rhetorical question, we weren't looking for an answer here. It seems your little girlfriend has chosen a side. She and her clan of misfits have aided in Michael, our greatest asset in keeping order in this madness, escape.

"As you know they somehow obtained a copy of Stella's notebook. However, we don't believe Michael and Asante have reunited as of yet. We don't know precisely what the notebook contains, but we know it contains the schematics for a weapon that could potentially destroy what we have known as reality since pretty much the dawn of civilization. Michael must not, under any circumstance, reach The Wave or be reunited with his daughters."

Fairchild began to squeeze his fist tightly and as he did, Brennan felt as if all the air in his lungs was being squeezed out of his body, he couldn't breathe.

"Do you understand the implications of what I'm telling you?"

Brennan did his best to nod his head yes. As he did, Fairchild opened his hand as if to release him. Brennan could feel the rush of air fill up his lungs. He gasped and took several deep breaths bringing life back into his body.

"But how do I intercept him? He's too smart to be found on grid. He could literally be anywhere. Not to mention, uh-hum," he coughed. "We don't know the location of Asante or any other Wave member. It literally is picking a needle out of a haystack."

"Not with the quantum computer. Schmidt should be able to assist." Farraday added dryly.

Not surprised, Brennan shot back, "You don't think she's going to give up any more information unless she is incentivized, do you?"

"Carmichael will assist you in that," at which point Carmichael entered the room. Then Farraday added, "We've decided that Carmichael will also accompany you from now until you find Michael. Just in case you were thinking of trying to betray us again, he will 'incentivize' you to stay on course."

*   *   *

Chelo and Asante had been hiking the mountains behind the Eslan Institute for an hour and a half. Asante wasn't sure what hiking had to do with *The Now*, but she was eager to find out.

They were climbing toward a peak and Chelo said, "Pay attention to your breath"

The only thing Asante knew about her breath at this moment was that she was out of it.

"A little further," Chelo encouraged.

Asante thought of herself as a fit person, but her thighs were on fire as she reached the little clearing at the peak of a mountain. She closed her eyes momentarily to prevent sweat from getting in them.

Suddenly, Chelo was at her side and whispered into her ear, "Keep your eyes closed, what do you hear?"

Asante replied with, "Nothing"

"Ok, let's start with your breath. I want you to concentrate on it, feel and imagine the air enter and fill your lungs. Feel your diaphragm expand and contract as you blow the air out again."

At first, Asante noticed nothing, then she could hear her and feel her breath in her body. Next, she could hear a hawk in the distance calling out. "I hear a hawk somewhere," She whispered.

"Good. Now open your eyes and let The Now in."

As she did, she noticed the sky and the clouds moving subtly, she could feel a gentle breeze against her skin, the leaves on the trees were vibrant and she could hear them dance in the wind, and the rolling mountains were majestic. The more connected she became with her breath, the more connected she became with all that she encountered. Her thoughts began to dissipate as her awareness of her body and everything she encountered rose from the depths of her consciousness. *The Now.* She looked at Chelo and she felt even more drawn to him than just a moment before.

"I'm here. I am present," she affirmed.

"What do you want to do?" He asked, smiling down at her and sharing in this wonderful moment.

"What I've wanted to do since I met you." She pulled him closer to her body by grabbing him by his belt buckle. He took her into his arms and they kissed in the reality of their love. A moment later they laid down and consummated their connection on top of the world.

*   *   *

"Douglas will win the election next month and we will be in a position to set The War in motion immediately. Our contacts are in place and are waiting for your command." Fairchild oozed as he shook the martini in the tumbler that he was making for himself and Farraday.

"Brennan will lead us to Asante, Aissa, and Michael but the question is the timeline. The likelihood of all three of their deaths occurring simultaneously will take a precise tactical schematic. We can't take the chance of leaving one of them alive because that one could galvanize The Wave to be a formative advisory in this war." Fairchild continued as he handed Farraday her drink.

"It doesn't matter, either way, as long as we kill Asante, there will be no hope."

"So, you do believe she's The Aurora?"

"Not necessarily but I'm not willing to take a chance at this point. If they believe it, we destroy their faith when we destroy her."

Chapter 16
Entrainment

Asante spent the better part of the next two months spending more and more time in *The Now*. She, Aissa, Marie, J.StaRR, and Massah started their days together in group meditation. This sharpened Asante's ability to get out of her thoughts and into the present more keenly. After morning meditations they would do yoga out on the cliffs followed by a hike. Marie would then prepare them lunch much like her grandmother used to do for the members of The Wave before her.

During lunch, the conversation always included a discussion on the sad state of affairs in the world. Asante was astonished every day by how much she didn't know about the world she had inhabited for thirty years. She learned of the grid which facilitated the veil over society. Banking records, online social media profiles, GPS, as well as many other facets of modern day living created the building blocks of the grid.

Superimposed on top of the grid are the many facets of the veil. False religion, education, capitalism, democracy; all used to prohibit, instead of their intended purpose of liberation. The discords that society has accepted as status quo, from racism and classism to poverty and malnutrition, all devised and perpetuated to keep the view of the masses filtered by the veil. What she had always assumed were fantasy ravings of conspiracy theorists had actual validity. Drugs *were* being flooded into impoverished neighborhoods, authorities *were* actually assassinating heroes and heroines that could shed light on the truth, all the while society marched forward complacent and complicit amongst these atrocities.

But in response, they only spoke of the new age, which they had no doubt was coming. All the problems of the world would not exist, but Asante noticed that there were no cohesive plans to get from point A to point B. There was no discussion of the mechanism which would facilitate society's evolution.

She didn't know if these discussions were happening solely for her benefit and the real planning was happening elsewhere but she was waiting for the right moment to bring it up with Aissa. It had been difficult to get one-on-one time with her. Asante was beginning to wonder if she was purposefully avoiding her. After lunch every day she seemed to disappear.

As they were clearing the plates, once lunch was finished Asante asked, "Can I talk to you?"

"About what?"

"A few things, but presently, why you've been avoiding me?"

Aissa smirked, as she began to walk out of the kitchen. "I'm not avoiding you, I'm just inundated with the all the moving parts of what we are aiming to do. Not all of which include you just yet."

Slightly offended but also curious, Asante continued, "Like what?"

"Like, you need to focus on being prepared and not what I'm doing." Aissa shot back as she left the room. Asante stood there not knowing how to feel.

The rest of the day Asante stayed in her room feeling annoyed at best and lost in her head. *So much for The Now*, she thought and *what was Aissa hiding?*

Despite what Aissa said, Asante was almost sure that whatever she was hiding had everything to do with her. A knock on her door interrupted her thoughts.

"Come in." She called out.

Marie stood in the doorway.

"You look and feel like you need a break, let's get out of here." She smiled, held up her car keys and dangled them in the air.

"Yes, yes that's exactly what I need!" Asante got out of the bed, grabbed a sweater and followed Marie out of the room. Marie had already pulled her car around which was parked out front when they walked outside. A teal green Volkswagen Beetle. It perfectly suited her. As Marie started the engine, Asante asked: "So where are we going?"

"Just a lounge, get you that blue cheese and olive dirty martini you've been craving, yeah?" She grinned. Asante didn't know if she'd ever get used to the idea of someone inside her mind. "Bad news is there's nothing around here, it's an hour away. But that'll give us time to chat." Marie said brightly. Asante smiled back. She was happy to get out.

The coast was breathtaking as the sun set behind them while they drove from Big Sur to the small town of Carmel. Marie was a lot of fun. She had a dry sense of humor which cracked Asante up. She could also do impressions of almost all the members of the wave. This had Asante laughing so hard her stomach hurt. She let go for the first time that she could remember. It eased the tension in her brain and allowed for a question to rise to the surface that she had forgotten about.

"I just remembered something that I wanted to ask about?" She offered as they stopped laughing at Marie's last impression.

"You want to know what you saw emanating from the city the night you were kidnapped from The Fairchild Estate?" Marie suggested.

"Yes, and does it have to do with entrainment or integration?" Asante queried as she adjusted to Marie's telepathic ability more quickly than she previously thought possible.

"For the lack of a better word you were visually interpreting the auras or waves in all of us. We all have energy fields, and you were able to see the projection of those fields from the people inhabiting San Francisco that night. It's because you were integrated that you were able to see the auras."

"Did they give me something to make me have the ability to see them?" Asante asked curiously.

"No, you've always had these abilities, everyone on the planet does. They are just dormant, waiting to be accessed.

"No, they probably gave you something that took away your inhibitions, which typically distract us from The Now. Once you are present your abilities are pretty easy to access. They more or less begin to flow through you.

"First, you'll notice the waves or chi in your body. Next, your senses will become heightened. As you reach higher levels of presence or integration, your attention will include a focus on the connection from within to the world around you.

"You will literally be able to pick a point in a frequency or wave in which you can ride and eventually wield," Marie explained.

"Well, I haven't seen auras since that night but I have integrated or been present, so what am I missing?"

"You are whole, Asante, lacking nothing. When you let The Now in—it offers possibility. You haven't experienced some higher levels of entrainment yet but that doesn't mean you haven't entrained or that you won't. And just because one moment offered the ability to align with auras, doesn't mean every moment will."

"What about this blowing in your ear that I've heard about? I don't exactly know what you are connecting with but trust it is something."

That hadn't occurred to Asante but it definitely felt accurate. She would begin to seek answers in her daily meditation.

The beetle began to slow down as they pulled up to a beautiful modern wood, steel, and glass hotel.

"Is this it?"

"Yes, you're going to love it, it's in the lobby of this Hyatt."

They got out and scaled what seemed like an endless amount of steps to the entrance. The lobby was stunning and led them to the lounge. It took Asante's breath away. Indoor/outdoor seating adorned plush cushions low to the ground. Stone and glass fire pits accented the space beautifully. Dimmed lighting and candles set the perfect ambiance.

Though they were impressed, they still headed straight for the bar.

"Two dirty blue cheese olive Martinis," Marie told the bartender.

"You just gave me life," Asante breathed in response. Moments later their drinks were ready. They held up their glasses and Asante found herself saying, "To The Now!"

Marie smiled and they sipped. "I like that, to The Now," Marie repeated.

"I know what's being asked of you, but what do you want of The Now?" Marie asked.

Asante was surprised by the question. So much had happened over the past few months, she hadn't asked herself that question in her new paradigm. Growing up and even during the pursuit of her career goals as a surgeon, it was very clear. Survive the horror that defined her early childhood and create a life where she would never experience that type of pain again. Now that she had chosen this new path she wasn't sure if her aims had changed.

"Haven't decided yet?" Marie answered for her.

Asante shook her head in response.

"Let's take in the view," Marie suggested. They got up and walked toward the infinity edge pool in the center of the room. There were glass balconies on each side with an exquisite view of the ocean.

Right before the indoor seating transitioned into outdoor seating, at a booth to Asante's right sat a couple. But as Asante connected eyes with the young woman, she realized that this was a young girl. Furthermore, Asante could feel she was in trouble. She turned to Marie as she reached the balcony, ready to speak, but Marie was already nodding in agreement.

She said, "I know."

Then Asante actually heard Marie's voice inside her head say, *follow my lead*. Marie then turned back and started walking toward the booth where the couple sat.

Before she reached them, Marie purposely tripped and spilled her drink on the man, who was clearly in his late forties. Asante got to the table as the man was brushing off Marie who was insisting on buying him a drink. The girl, who had too much make-up on in order to mask her age was given away by her sheer panic at Marie's presence. She now looked like a terrified little girl of no more than twelve or thirteen years of age.

"It's really not necessary, Miss, please never mind the accident." The man stumbled over his words as Marie and Asante sat in front of them. The girl's eyes were a mixture of emotions, pleading for help but frightened to death of the repercussions.

Marie spoke first. "Now we can do this one of two ways, you can get up and leave this child in our care and no one has to know, or everyone can know and you can leave here in handcuffs."

The man immediately looked down into his lap as if contemplating his options. But when he lifted his head, the look of malicious intent couldn't be denied as a smug grin crept across his lips.

"I think you ladies have misunderstood the situation and your options, so I'll make it crystal clear." He smiled, as he pulled out a police badge and placed it on the table. "You can get up from this table of your own free will or you can walk out of here in cuffs and in a whole world of trouble."

Before he could finish spewing his threat or Marie could respond, Asante could feel the rush of wind blow into her ears, remembering Marie's words from their conversation earlier, she consciously felt herself become a part of the wind.

The next few moments would change her forever. She reached across the table and grabbed the man's hand. Asante felt the wind rush through her entire body and flow through her hand and fingers. She began to hold the man's hand tighter. As she did she could feel heat emanating from the palm of her hand and flow out of her fingertips but it didn't harm her. He tried to pull his arm away as the warmth from her hand and fingers turned into an intense fire. His hand and arm began to turn red and white as the current ran up his arm and attacked his entire body. He was sweating, red, and scared. It was as if he were burning up from the inside out.

"Do you want to come with us?" Marie asked the girl, who stared in disbelief as tears rolled down her cheeks. She nodded her head in agreement.

At this, she crawled out under the table because the man's body was blocking her exit. She and Marie left the booth. Asante remained. Still holding his one hand, she stared into his bulging eyes. All of her anger and pain released into his body.

She wasn't going to let him hurt that child anymore. She would stop him and those like him from hurting the innocent. He began to convulse as people started to stare in the direction of the booth. She then heard a clear, yet unfamiliar voice in her mind, almost in the wind rushing through her body: *Asante, stop, let him go*. But she couldn't. She wouldn't. Blood started to trickle from his eyes, nose, and mouth. *Asante let him go!* She refused. Then someone started to scream and panic broke out in the lounge. In the midst of the chaos, Asante finally let go of his lifeless hand. She got up and slowly walked out as if in a trance.

When she reached the entrance of the lobby Marie's screams grounded her and she descended the steps in moments. Asante jumped into the beetle. The sounds of sirens numbed and blocked out the words coming out of Marie's mouth as the three of them drove into the night.

Chapter 17
Brennan

Just when Brennan began to fear for his life because his search for Michael had led nowhere, his Asante was his saving grace. While eating his room service breakfast he decided to find something on television to distract himself from his imminent doom. Carmichael was still asleep in the queen bed adjacent to his own, so he muted the volume. But as he flipped through the channels he stopped on CNN's red breaking news banner because of the headline—"Caramel Sheriff murdered in local lounge, surgeon wanted for questioning." Then he saw her. Someone had recorded her on their phone. The video showed Asante as she got up from a table and slowly walked out of a lounge. The camera then panned back to the table where a man sat with blood streaming out of every orifice on his face covered in boils.

A moment later Carmichael's phone rang. He woke immediately and answered. "Yes, ma'am, no, no. Yes, right away," he replied, then hung up the phone. Brennan turned to face him. He stared at the television. "Seems it's your lucky day. Though Schmidt wouldn't help you find Michael, looks like your girlfriend will do the trick." Carmichael got up, pointed to the television and walked into the bathroom.

Dr. Schmidt wasn't happy when Brennan had returned to her empty-handed and had asked for more favors.

She left him with, "This time I'll do my own bidding."

This frightened Brennan and had him immediately fear for Asante's life. And although he was happy to have a lead on Asante for his own fate, he needed to devise a plan to ensure Asante could join him possibly away from The Sephiren and The Wave, if necessary.

"What's the plan?" He called out to Carmichael in the bathroom.

"Don't you worry your pretty little head about that, Brennan. When the time is right you'll be asked to do what's necessary. Until then enjoy the ride."

He was definitely out of the loop. He would have to come up with something proactively and seize the moment when it presented itself. He hoped Asante would be ready for him because it might come down to her life or his own.

*   *   *

"Then to top it off you bring this child here!" Aissa screamed at the top of her lungs as she paced back and forth. Though it was three am, all the members of The Wave were present in the great room in the main house at the Eslan Institute. Asante was still in a trance-like state. She had never known the power she felt that flowed through her while she sat at that table. It was freedom, but her unwillingness to control it cost someone their life. Her rationale would have her believe he deserved it for what he was doing to the child that now sat beside her, but her higher-self knew that was wrong. She was a murderer and she would now have to deal with that reality.

"Marie, how could you let this happen? Have you been teaching her to entrain without my knowledge? How can she be so powerful to take a life with such ease and mastery within moments?" Aissa asked.

"No, of course not. I only described the process to her a few moments earlier...it all happened so fast. I wasn't even sure what she was doing until it was too late." Marie explained completely still disheveled.

"The same way she was able to give life during that surgery without knowledge of any of this," Nyrraw interjected, "because, she is The Aurora." Suddenly Asante was brought back to the moment. Everyone in the room's eyes on her.

"Now more than ever she must be protected. We need to demonstrate love and patience with her. Not frustration and scrutiny, Aissa." Nyrraw continued, "She obviously is more powerful than any of us imagined and her connection to The Now is deeper than we thought possible, so let's seek to understand before we seek to be understood."

"That's all well and good but know The Sephiren will be at our doorstep in twelve hours or less, so yeah, there's that!" Aissa said, not backing down.

Chelo then moved to the center of the group and put his hand on Asante's shoulder. "If I may, placing blame and contemplating the enemy's next move isn't going to serve us. Neither is coddling Asante. We need to be proactive. There's always a solution in The Now, so let's find it. We don't have Michael nor can we read the notebook, but we have what they both point to. Asante."

Asante was filled with so many emotions at this moment. The disappointment in her sister's countenance was literally breaking her already wounded heart. While the looks of uncertainty in everyone else added to her anxious mind. But then she looked into the eyes of the young girl that sat beside her. There she found hope. This girl had known only pain for as long as she could remember and for the first time new possibility was on the horizon. All was not lost. Asante cleared her throat.

"I am not sure of what to do next, and my heart is heavy with making a horrible choice last night, but Chelo's right, we have The Now. Which means we not only have me but each other. We are the most powerful people on the planet, so how can we create hope in this moment, because if we can't, how can we expect her to do so," pointing to the young girl, "or anyone else still cloaked in the pain of the veil?"

"So, what do you suggest, oh fearless leader?" Aissa joked, half mocking her as well as challenging her to step up.

"Michael," Asante said nearly whispering, as the blowing in her ears had returned.

"Yeah, we know we need to find him. That's what we've been up to, but he obviously doesn't want to be found." Aissa fired, not hiding her exasperation.

Asante could see a beach in her mind's eyes as the wind began to rush into her ears again. She allowed her being to become a part of it, and at first, she could only hear familiar laughter. She closed her eyes and in front of her was a beach, with her, her pregnant mother, and Michael on a picnic blanket. She heard Stella say, "I just love when we come to Pismo." Michael then looked directly at her and smiled. Then as if the memory were made of sand—the image of the beach and the three of them disappeared as if blown away by the wind. Asante opened her eyes.

"You're right, Aissa, he wants me to find him and I know where he is."

*　　　*　　　*

A team from The Sephiren met Carmichael and Brennan two hours earlier and escorted them to a private airport in Los Angeles. But when they got to the hanger, outside was a military Kamov KA-50 fueled up and loaded with even more ammunition.

They had been flying for an hour, and the eight other men besides himself and Carmichael loaded their weapons and got ready to descend from the helicopter. Brennan recognized the Eslan Institute on the cliffs below.

"I thought we were detaining Asante in order to trap Michael," Brennan said into his headset.

"Nope, new orders, shoot to kill. Everyone, especially the Argueta sisters." Carmichael's voice blared in Brennan's headset. Brennan felt like the air had been knocked out of his chest. He found himself praying she had already escaped.

*　　　*　　　*

After loading all supplies and weaponry that everyone could carry on their person the members of The Wave sat in a circle inside Eslan and began to focus their energy on protecting the space they were in. They knew that The Sephiren would be coming shortly. They also knew they didn't have enough time to escape without leaving their tracks on the grid. Their only hope was to stand their ground and combat whatever force The Sephiren would send in order to buy time to escape safely without a trace. The idea was to create a force field around, not only the main house but all of the grounds leading up into the Santa Lucia Mountains. From there teams would split up and rendezvous once they found Michael. Everyone was anxious because a force field of this magnitude had never been attempted. But there was hope as well because they never had Asante before.

Nyrraw led the group meditation. His experience as a pastor allowed for him to guide the collective energy in the room with mastery.

"Now that you've created this formless, impenetrable space in your minds, give it form and imagine it first protecting your bodies, now let it grow to protect this house, now the grounds, now the entire mountain range. Now rise and walk out of this space with the complete faith that you are protected and will not be harmed by any weapon formed against you!" As they rose, they could hear a helicopter approaching.

"They are here," Nyrraw affirmed their fears out loud.

"This clearing right outside the main house is the best place for contact, get ready to descend." Brennan heard the unit leader say in his headset. His heart began to race. But before anyone could descend from the helicopter the large doors to the main house opened and people started to stream out of the house.

"Abort, looks like they are going to make this easy, launch aerial arsenal, load guns!"

The helicopter then opened fire at the people coming out of the house on the ground. The bullets began to ricochet off of what appeared to be some type of invisible force field. Realizing what was happening, Carmichael began to focus on penetrating the shield.

The unit leader screamed. "Hit them with all we got!"

The gunfire sounded like fireworks to Asante as she took her first step out of the house. She was the last out of the house and everyone in front of her was running for cover in the trees on the other side of the driveway some thousand feet in front of her. Although she wanted to run her instinct was to walk. She took each step as consciously as she could. Something was disrupting the force field. She could feel it. She stopped halfway to the other side and looked directly into the sky at the helicopter and incoming gunfire. The shield blocked all of it and created a spectacular light show of beautiful color. For a moment Asante was lost in its ironic aesthetic. Then she saw him in the door of the aircraft looking directly at her. She felt him more than she could actually make out his person in all the light and smoke. Brennan.

He saw Asante exit the house last. His breath caught in his chest. When she stopped in the middle of the clearing, at first, he wondered what she was doing. Then he heard her in his head as clear as if she were standing next to him. *Hi,* Asante said, simply.

Hi, he replied. None of the things he dreamt of saying to her came to mind. Then a moment or two of silence.

Funny meeting you here, Asante joked finally breaking the tension.

Brennan laughed out loud as a tear rolled down his cheek. Carmichael's voice in his headset interrupted him before he could reply.

"Keep her focused on you. I'm almost through the force field, load missile for a direct shot at her," he continued to the pilot.

Brennan knew this moment would come, *I want you to know that I did love you and still do,* he thought.

Asante answered back with, *You were my everything, but what does it matter now?*

"A moment longer," Carmichael said.

"Waiting for your go," the pilot responded.

What does it matter now, matter now, matter now? Asante's question rang in his head. It did.

Asante! RUN, RUN NOW! He screamed out with all the fabric of his being.

At the same time, Carmichael yelled "now!" Was he too late? Asante looked up at the helicopter and directly into his soul. Instead of running, she stood squarely in the direction of the helicopter and opened her arms, stretching them wide into the air as if she were welcoming the incoming threat. Brennan watched helplessly as the missile left the craft and headed toward her. But just at the moment of impact, instead of blowing up his precious love, a smaller force field surrounded her body and absorbed the energy of the missile. The light of it shined brightly like a star on the ground. The light of energy became smaller and smaller until it was small enough for Asante to hold it in her hand. She smiled, then threw it back in the direction of the helicopter. It was the last light that Brennan saw before he lost consciousness.

Asante was breathing so heavily that she could barely catch her breath as the helicopter exploded into thousands of pieces in mid-air. Everyone hiding in the trees ran out to meet her.

Aissa was the first to speak, "Ok-k-k, rockstar, are you kidding me! You ARE THE AURORA!" Everyone surrounded them with love and appreciation.

*   *   *

Nothing. Complete darkness. As Brennan's conscious mind began to wake, this was all he could experience. He then remembered the light and opened his eyes. He could see the night's stars through the trees above him. He looked around. He could feel his body. He attempted to move. He was completely unharmed. Not a scratch. In the clearing through the trees, he could see the wreckage from the helicopter still burning. *Asante*. She had saved him.

Chapter 18
Quantum

"Dr. Farraday," The guard greeted Emily by name when she entered the lobby of Quanta.

She thought of all the roads she had chosen to lead her to this moment. Emily had never been satisfied with what was given to her. She would rather prefer what she could take. Since she was a child she had rebelled against the very notion of second place. It's why she left her family and The Wave when they insisted on her living in the shadows. She was destined for more. It's why she rose very quickly through the ranks of The Sephiren and it's why she would win this war over the fate of humanity. And no one, not Asante, or Aissa, Michael, Fairchild, nor Schmidt would get in her way. Especially not Schmidt, especially not today.

The elevator chimed and opened. Dr. Schmidt smiled at Emily, meeting her gaze over her spectacles, lowered down her nose. "I thought we could walk down Sunset and chat. It's such a lovely day." Schmidt said before Emily could speak.

Emily moved aside and replied, "After you." Realizing she had been slightly outmaneuvered by Schmidt, she decided to play along. "You knew I was coming, did the computer tell you why as well?" Emily said as she put on her Gucci sunglasses to protect against the midday sun's rays reflecting off the mirrored buildings.

"If I had asked it but I don't need the quantum computer to give me answers to the obvious. It's the probability of the unseen that it's most useful in determining." Schmidt replied with a smirk on her lips. "The real query here," she continued, "is will you ask the question that will give you the best probability of what you want to see happen?"

"Where is Michael?"

"We could ask quantum that, but let me ask you a question, Farraday, what do you want?"

A myriad of images flooded Emily's mind; Aissa, Michael, and Asante's demise for one, unlimited power and mankind kneeling at her feet, a cat? But she was clearly not going to give Schmidt anything that might run contrary to her own musings. Schmidt had made it clear with Brennan that she had ulterior motives and she ran the Quanta sub-faction with complete autonomy. She couldn't be trusted.

"I want to put an end to this uprising attempting to disrupt the natural order of the world," Emily replied as a matter of fact.

"Which means?" Schmidt prodded.

"We need to destroy The Wave!" Emily answered quickly.

"So what question do you want to ask Quantum?" Schmidt asked as they had finished their walk around the block and had returned to the entrance of Quanta.

"How do we eradicate The Wave?" Emily said with fire in her eyes.

"Now that, Farraday, is an enterprising and profitable question. Let's go down and find out, yeah?"

As they entered the room where Quantum was located. Emily could feel the raw power of the machine. It was hard for her to contain her excitement though she knew she must.

"The sheer possibility of what the mind can create as an extension of itself is astounding." Schmidt offered as they sat down at the console.

Emily smiled in agreement. As Schmidt began to type their mutually agreed upon query. Emily began to focus on what she had learned from all the years experimenting on Michael. Through many years of effort, she was able to mimic the process of entrainment by accessing all the same faculties that The Wave philosophy pointed to, minus the intent to live harmoniously with all one encounters, but rather control and manipulate all that one encounters. She began to entrain Quantum mentally. And as she did, she metaphysically understood what lay before her. She knew she must act fast. Schmidt was smiling at her as she pressed enter, sending their question to Quantum. Her smile quickly turned into a look of terror and panic as she met Emily's eyes. She lifted her arms to create a shield to block the incoming energy gathering behind Emily's irises. But it was too late, the bolt of electricity traveled the length of her entire body by the time her arms were in mid-air. Her lifeless body collapsed into a pile of ash a moment later.

*   *   *

The three-hour ride from Eslan to Pismo Beach seemed to fly by in moments. Though it was a challenge to get out of Big Sur off-grid because the authorities were in search of Asante. There were several checkpoints where Marie had to "Jedi Mind-Trick" some officers into not recognizing Asante's face. Most of the members of The Wave decided to move forward with their plan of refuge in the Santa Lucia Mountain range, while J.StaRR and The Misfitz flew to San Francisco for a concert. The small group that accompanied Asante to Pismo were speculating the entire ride about her abilities as if she were not present.

"She is literally The Weapon that will be used against The Sephiren in order to free humankind." Aissa was saying.

"We don't know that. I think it is prudent to hear what insight Michael has to offer once we know for sure what the notebook says, Aissa." Nyrraw retorted quickly.

"I just think either way she's a badass and I'm glad she's with us!" Marie chimed in, almost giddy with laughter.

"Agreed." Chelo and Obadias affirmed in unison.

Asante was thrilled that she was able to access what she apparently was intended for, but she couldn't help but feel like she was missing an integral piece in all of this. The part of her that saved Brennan, not because he *deserved* it, but because it was in opposition to the part of her that took that sheriff's life, was somehow connected. As if it were from the same source. But how could good and evil, pain and love, all be coming from the same place? Wasn't this notion in opposition to what The Wave theory pointed to? She needed understanding.

*   *   *

The exit for Pismo Beach City Limits was coming up. Asante began to focus on her father and searched for a direction that felt like his energy was emanating from. Again, the wind. But this time she could feel it pulling her.

As they exited the highway, Asante said, "I'll direct you from here, make a left at the light." After traveling about three miles west. They saw signs for Avila Beach. "Exit here," Asante instructed as the wind intensified and pulled her in the direction of the beach. When they arrived oceanfront, they were greeted by a tourists' enclave. Hotels, shops, boardwalk, and a pier were filled with people. "This doesn't feel familiar." Asante admitted, "But I know he's here."

"Hiding in plain sight?" Aissa suggested.

A moment later they all got out of the van and stretched. Asante was immediately overwhelmed by the number of people everywhere. She could feel and see their auras so clearly now that at first, it frightened her. Her building panic was interrupted by Marie's soothing voice.

"Breathe. What you are experiencing isn't separate from yourself. Be a part of it, find the connections, we are all one, one Source experienced in various forms."

Asante took a deep clearing breath, as she did, she relaxed into The Now becoming one with all that she encountered. She was immediately drawn to the ocean.

"Let's spread out," Chelo suggested. Asante agreed though she knew where she was going.

A few minutes later, Asante found herself changing into a wetsuit that she rented along with a surfboard. She left the surf shop awkwardly carrying the board. She had never surfed a day in her life. Yet here she was dragging this board through the sand heading for the ocean. She got into the water and managed her way onto it and began to paddle. Asante did not know where she was going, but the wind kept pulling her further and further into the ocean. All of a sudden the blowing stopped and all was still. Asante turned around on the board and faced the shoreline. She was a good half mile away from the beach. The closest surfers were some thousand feet away. She waited. After about twenty minutes she decided to turn over on her back and face the sky. She couldn't find a cloud. The sky was clear and beautiful. She found so much peace in allowing herself to connect with the view above her.

Asante, are you ready to ride the wave? She could hear her father's soft voice in her mind. She smiled and slowly turned over to find her dad treading water as he held on to the front of her board, with only his curly black hair, eyes, and nose visible. She jumped off of the board and into his arms. As they embraced, she felt as if she had left her body and her being merged with his. As she looked into his eyes, his deep dimples seemed to tickle her soul. Daddy. Lost but now found. Anything was possible now.

*   *   *

After debriefing the sub-faction at Quanta regarding the unfortunate fate of Dr. Elouise Schmidt, Emily directed all supervisors to begin reporting daily to the San Francisco Division of The Sephiren. The fear in their eyes exhilarated Emily's already building excitement. She mandated that the Quantum computer would exclusively be used by her with no exception. They reset all the security measures to her specific biometrics. Though these measures were more for preventing anyone else from tampering with the machine while it was in her control. Now that she could mentally access the mainframe her connection to the Quantum computer would keep her a step ahead of The Wave and ultimately crown her the victor in this war.

After strategizing for several hours on Fairchild's private jet back to San Francisco, Emily realized the error of her own assumptions. For a while, the eradication of The Wave seemed impossible. Every time she sought her desired end, the paths that Quantum offered to attain it also offered too many possibilities for it to slip through her fingers. The more she tried to control all the factors the more elusive certain triumph became. She had to change the variables upon which the algorithm was based. She had been picking this thing up with the wrong handle. We don't need to make the choice for mankind, mankind will choose order over freedom if given the option, she finally concluded.

She dialed Fairchild, "We have a new aim, one which will accomplish our goals more efficiently."

"I hear your Quanta trip was successful. Is the Argueta girl not who we are after?"

"No, she's still the key, but in delivering mankind into our grasps in a way that has never been truly accomplished by The Sephiren before us," Emily replied, almost beside herself.

"Ah, brilliant," Fairchild said greedily.

"Bring me their Star! We'll need to draw them out for the world to see."

Chapter 19
J.StaRR

J.StaRR could hear and feel the music coming from the ballroom at the Filmore from backstage. Her opening act, Sylvan Esso, was the perfect set up for her performance and their fans. However, she and the members of The Misfitz couldn't give anything much attention, considering what they had seen Asante do less than twenty-four hours ago. Normally, they were focused on their set and the intention they wanted to bring forth during the show for their fans. Usually, J.StaRR would focus their energy, by opening in prayer, then they would collectively meditate on their intention. Today their excitement couldn't be contained.

"We will literally be unstoppable with what she's capable of," Mystro said nearly skipping from one side of the dressing room to the other.

"And when she opened her arms as if to say bring it, to the incoming missile, I thought for sure, she's lost it and it was all over," Kaz added.

"Not me," Chase Money continued, "I knew she had to be The Aurora. She's Aissa's older sister and look how dope she is."

J.StaRR was just as enthused as her band members, but ever since they touched down in San Francisco she's had the feeling they were being followed. Her stomach had been in knots from her first step into the venue. She kept her eyes out for anything outside of the norm. They had played the Filmore at least a half-dozen times. So she was very familiar with the procedure, sound check, and layout of the place. Nothing had caught her attention, but something was wrong, she could feel it. It was about twenty-five minutes until their set, so she'd better focus The Misfitz or there would be no show.

"So what do we want to put forth tonight in lieu of out newfound inspiration? Power, faith, truth? What do you guys think, and fast, we've been caught up and the show is about to start."

"What about hope?" Kaz asked enthusiastically.

They all looked at each other in agreement, nodding in affirmation. They closed their eyes and began to meditate on hope;

for the show, for the fans, and for the world. There was a reason to celebrate tonight and they were set on jamming as hard as they could to commemorate the new hope planted in their hearts.

*   *   *

Sitting across the table from her father at The Blue Moon Diner felt surreal. Michael wanted some one-on-one time with Asante before they joined the others. However, the last twenty minutes were filled with very few actual words. Michael was mostly quiet as he stared into her soul.

Finally, she asked, "What do you see?"

He smiled deeply, looked down into his lap for a moment, then as if speaking to her heart said, "I see the hope of Stella, not just as it relates to humanity, but as a beautiful, accomplished woman, capable of our greatest gift, love. It runs through you fervently, it's why you are The Aurora. No matter what the answer to a problem seems to be, remember that love is the greatest power that The Now offers."

"I wish it were that simple to me. People are dying literally and figuratively every day, and I'm not clear on how something as esoteric as love is going to save them from the very real tangible threat of The Sephiren on their lives?" Asante was almost hyperventilating at the thought of it.

"You will," Michael responded simply.

Almost as if on cue Aissa, Obadias, Chelo, Marie, and Nyrraw walked into the diner.

When Michael looked up, he was stuck, after a few moments of watching the group approach the table, he uttered "Stella," as he took in Aissa's countenance.

Aissa, not expecting to feel such a rush of emotion was overwhelmed at the sight of her father. He rose and caught her in his arms, just as her legs gave out under the weight of the moment. She collapsed into the love of her father's embrace. After a few moments of burying her head in his chest, she lifted her eyes to meet his gaze.

104

"That's what they say, Daddy, that I'm her twin, is it true?"

"Except for those flecks of gold in your eyes that you obviously got from your old man, you're the spitting image of her," Michael said fondly looking down at her.

As they sat down introductions were made. Although, at this moment the whole table was in awe of Michael, the man at the helm of The Wave's freedom fighting. Obadias, Chelo, Marie, and Nyrraw felt like they were meeting their childhood hero as did Asante and Aissa in their own way.

Aissa, of course, jumped right in, "So when do you think you can start decoding Mommy's journal?"

"No need. I already know what it says and the proof of it is sitting right in front of me," Michael replied.

"So Asante is The Aurora?" Aissa asked quickly.

"You and everyone at this table know the answer to that question, with the exception of Asante."

Everyone simultaneously shifted their attention to Asante, who now looked "caught".

Michael continued, "She will in time, but what we must figure out is how to protect the one you call the Star? The Sephiren is launching a new strategy and they will use that girl as the catalyst."

"When?" Aissa asked concerned about her best friend.

"Unfortunately my dear, right now."

* * *

In the middle of J.StaRR's first song, "Energy," is when she first noticed it. Normally when she and The Misfitz performed she could see the sound waves in an array of dancing beams of light-- almost like lasers leave the stage and flow into the audience. But for the first time ever it seemed as though a teenage boy in the second row, center from the stage could see the waves as well. While trying to focus on singing J.StaRR noticed the boy pointing to a specific frequency traveling through the air above him. The girl next to him began to point. A few more people.

Then it spread through the audience in the ballroom like fire. Everyone stopped paying attention to the stage and looked at the amazing light show in the air. J.StaRR and The Misfitz began to look at each other in confusion. How was the audience able to simultaneously see this reality? Then J.StaRR saw them, in the hands of just about everyone in the room was a small paper cup with the sponsored logo *Transverse Media*. Had The Sephiren drugged the audience? That's when she noticed the cameras. They had drugged the audience and were about to film what would ultimately end in chaos. She remembered Asante's account of what happened at The Fairchild Estate. J.StaRR could feel the panic building in the venue.

Usually, once the crowd was in the moment with the music and J.StaRR and The Misfitz, the waves would begin to permeate their beings, but the only thing the audience was aware of was how good the music and experience made them feel. Now, thrust into this seemingly mind-bending experience with no warning, the crowd was having a very different reaction. Fear became palpable and began to emanate from each person in the room.

J.StaRR turned her head away from the mic and shouted to The Misfitz, "Stop playing, they can't see what we don't play and we've got to get out of here."

She then heard someone shout, "They drugged us, they drugged us!" As J.StaRR and The Misfitz tried to leave the stage pandemonium broke out. A literal stampede followed. People were trampling over one another as they attempted to exit the ballroom all at once. By the time they got back to the dressing room, the approaching sirens could be heard. Smoke started to funnel in under the dressing room door.

"Oh shit the joint is on fire!" Chase Money yelled. "We need to get out of here stat, check the doorknob and see if it's hot." He continued.

J.StaRR stepped in between the door and the guys, "There are people out there who are hurt that we can help. Let's be who we say we are, The Wave." She checked the door and stepped out into the hallway. A billow of smoke entered the room as the guys followed J.StaRR and stepped into the hallway barely able to see a foot in front of them.

By the time they reached the ballroom, it was completely ablaze. They began to check the bodies of people strewn about for life. There were a few people by the entrance calling out for survivors into the fire. Chase Money, Kaz, and Mystro carried ten people to safety.

J.StaRR told them to get out while she searched for any others. Then she saw him. It was the same teenage boy that first saw the sound wave above him. He was trapped underneath some sound equipment that had toppled over by the weight of the rushing crowd. She tried to move the soundboard but couldn't get enough leverage. She needed to move the ground. J.StaRR began to hum, as she did, she focused on the tectonic plates in the earth. The key was to be precise, to shift the plates just enough and focus the energy on this specific place. The ground beneath her feet began to move; the building around them shook. One more slight shift and she pushed with her whole self and moved it just enough to slide out. The young boy draped his arm around her shoulders as The Misfitz ran back in to help. They were all greeted by first responders at the entrance to the Filmore. The firemen brought them a few feet away to the paramedics for treatment.

Moments later J.StaRR was getting respiratory treatment for smoke inhalation when four officers approached the back of the ambulance. J.StaRR immediately thought, *Here we go*. But she said, "How may I help you, officers?"

*   *   *

It had been forty-eight hours since J.StaRR's arrest. The Misfitz were initially held for a few hours then released without the police ever questioning them. They had all reunited at an old Wave outpost at Canyon Ranch in Tucson, Arizona. Michael's premonition was unfolding as they all watched the TV screen in awe and disbelief. All the news cycles were running the story: *"Pop Star, secretly part of cult, drugs audience, stampede and fire ensue, twelve dead, one-hundred-thirty-four injured."*

MSNBC was advertising a Rachel Maddow exclusive interview with Dr. Emily Farraday, who reportedly has had many patients involved with the cult known as The Wave, in a few hours. And would offer insight into their aims.

Asante stared at the television displaying Dr. Farraday's face. She could feel anger building in her body.

Aissa entered the room, "What is that bitch up to?" She spat.

"Your aunt prides herself on always being one step ahead." Michael offered, shaking his head in regret.

"Our what?" Aissa and Asante shouted in unison.

"Emily Farraday is my sister. She left home at fourteen and changed her identity. To this day I don't know how she has seemingly not aged since the day she left all those years ago or how she got involved with The Sephiren, but even as a child she was cunning, manipulative and cold. She was behind imprisoning me, murdering your mother, kidnapping Asante, all of it, and I'm sure the list goes on. To answer your question, she's going to make them choose."

"Who?" Again, Asante and Aissa asked simultaneously.

"Everyone."

Chapter 20
Nyrraw

Jesus had always been the catalyst in Nyrraw's journey to The Now. His father David had instilled so much faith in him and his younger sister, Joi, during his sermon's as children, that even though his father's work with The Wave would eventually take him away from his duties as a pastor. The seed in their hearts was sown. Nyrraw as a teenager similarly would step away from The Wave and start his own Christian ministry called The Souls of Zion. He would utilize Jesus' messages to demonstrate the power that lies within all of us. He understood that when Jesus said, "Whoever believes in me will do the works I have been doing, and they will do even greater things than these," He was pointing man in the same direction as The Wave. If Jesus was the catalyst for his own journey he felt it could be for others. But when his father died and he realized that Joi had taken a more integral role within The Wave he knew he must return.

He had spent much of the last forty-eight hours in prayer and meditation. However, he was still battling himself on how to approach Joi's arrest, which now felt more like a kidnapping, as no one had heard from her. The Wave's informants in law enforcement couldn't seem to locate her anywhere. Michael nor Marie could sense her on a telepathic level. Nyrraw only had his faith to rely on now to quell his building anxiety, anger, and fear. However, he was clear that if she had been hurt or worse by The Sephiren, that all the meditation and prayer in the universe would be needed to thwart his vengeance. He was lost in his thoughts when he joined the others.

Everyone had gathered around the large flat screen TV in the recreational room at Canyon Ranch. The Rachel Maddow show had just begun. After Rachel's account of what happened at the Filmore, detailing the death and injured toll, she introduced Dr. Emily Farraday to give insight into the "cult," that J.StaRR apparently was acting on behalf of.

"So what differentiates this cult from other groups we've heard of in the past?" Rachel asked.

The camera zoomed in on Farraday's face, "The biggest distinction is that they can actually do what they claim." Farraday said coolly.

"Ok, what does that mean? What do they claim? Communication with God, aliens…what are we talking here?"

"They claim to have the ability to manipulate the elements that make up our known universe. Everything from electromagnetic and sound waves to very tangible elements like the earth and water." Farraday stated with the same calm resolve.

Rachel looked confused for a moment, then continued. "I'm sorry, I just want to be clear here about what you are saying. So these people, for a lack of a better word, claim to have superhuman abilities and it's true?"

"Not exactly, not superhuman, more like uber-human. They claim these abilities are accessible by all human beings. Which we don't believe to be true, but I have seen examples of it during my many years studying members of this group at Farraday Research and Laboratories." Farraday didn't so much as blink as the words left her lips.

Rachel stammered a bit, then finally collected herself and managed, "Well do you have any proof of your assertions outside of your word?"

At this, Farraday smiled broadly and said, "I thought you'd never ask. My associate Fairchild, should have just handed your producer a flash drive that contains footage that will answer your question."

Rachel nodded into the camera. "Roll tape?" Rachel said throwing her hands up.

A moment later a much younger version of Michael appeared on the screen. A title in the left-hand corner read "September 24, 1998, Sing Sing Correctional Facility, Psychiatric Ward-Farraday Research and Laboratories, Case # 0142, Experiment #9."

Michael sat at a desk with wires that had sensors placed on his head. A television was next to him facing the camera. A moment later a lab assistant came into view and turned on the television. A morning news broadcast was on the TV. Then Dr. Farraday's raspy voice could be heard though she was off-camera.

"Michael disrupt the broadcast."

Michael nodded in what seemed to be a trance-like state, closed his eyes, and a moment later the screen of the television displayed static or white noise. Off-camera again, Farraday's voice is heard.

"Re-establish transmission."

Instantly, the television was back on the news broadcast. The anchorman with his hand on his earpiece apologized for the technical difficulties and continued to report the news.

Once again off-camera, Farraday's voice is heard, "Disrupt the broadcast again but for precisely 10 seconds this time."

Again Michael closed his eyes and the screen displayed white noise. Only this time he counted out loud to ten upon which the broadcast resumed. Again, the news anchor apologized for the disruption but looked far more confused.

"Ok, Michael, one last test; disrupt all one hundred twenty-five stations that are broadcasting right now."

The television once again returned to black and white snow, the lab assistant once again stepped into view and flipped through all one hundred twenty-five channels using a remote control. All were white noise.

"Stop." Dr. Farraday ordered. A broadcast of "Live! With Regis and Kathy Lee" displayed on the TV screen, and again confusion had ensued regarding the broadcast. They were in the midst of collecting themselves and regaining control of the show when the lab assistant turned off the television.

"This concludes experiment number nine."

The television screen went black for a moment in the recreation room at Canyon Ranch, and then a close up of Rachel Maddow looking astonished. The camera panned out to reveal Farraday looking as smug as ever.

After a moment, Rachel said, "I'm not sure what to make of what we have just seen. My instinct wants to disbelieve. However, it is clear that this would be too much of an elaborate hoax. I guess my first question is, are they dangerous?"

Emily Farraday replied, "Yes, and we are now working with authorities to detain them. My understanding is that J.StaRR has been sent to Guantanamo Bay Detainment Camp for questioning and observation. But I'm sorry Rachel, this is all that we can disclose at this time. We are working with authorities who only authorized informing the public of the power they wield and the dangerous terroristic threat that they are to our way of life. In the next few hours, we will be releasing the known identities of the members that are still at large. That is all for now."

Emily Farraday then removed her mic, stood up and walked out of the studio.

Nyrraw turned off the television as Rachel began her sign-off remarks. He stood in front of the others with flames building behind his eyes.

"We've got to go get her!" He said, almost pleading.

"That's what they are expecting us to do, it will incite an all-out war. Guantanamo is a naval base. Are you prepared to attack the United States Government?" Michael asked.

With steel in his eyes, Nyrraw replied as though there was no other option, "Yes!"

"With what army? There's only two dozen of us or so that are capable of walking into that type of battle." Obadias interjected.

"Wait, let's think this thing through? What are they really after?" Aissa asked.

"To destroy our hope for humanity. To make The Wave an unviable option. That's why she's exposing us, and why they are using terms like *cult* to describe us and *manipulate* to describe our relationship to the elements around us. They want to cut us off at the pass; stop our movement before it has the possibility to offer a new way for man to exist." Michael said, giving his insight.

"How do we counter that? Expose them?" Aissa offered.

Everyone was silent for a moment or two searching each other's faces for an answer.

"Humankind is too entrenched into the fabric of what The Sephiren has created to ever believe that they are victims of their own volition, participating in the deception that masks their reality.

"No, what we must do is figure out a way to demonstrate who we really are and rescue J.StaRR in the process," Asante offered. Her words seemed to settle and calm the group. Now, all she had to do was figure out what she was talking about.

Chapter 21 The War
Part 1

A list of all known members and associates of The Wave were being broadcast by every major television station in the country. The list totaled precisely four hundred forty-four people spread throughout the world, most of which were in the United States. Americans seemed to be dividing; the majority immediately fell into the trap that The Sephiren devised. Fear was rampant amongst this group. Hotlines had been set up where people could call and report citizens in their community that they suspected to be members of The Wave.

There were protests calling for the deaths of all Wave members in every major city. But from a smaller group, there was compassion, empathy, and interest building for The Wave. Home videos of members doing miraculous, generous acts, like healing and saving lives were all over the internet. Images of peaceful arrests of Wave members were also pouring in. Family and friends of those arrested were using social media to question the legality and authenticity of these arrests.

A special investigation was launched by the Senate to quell the concerns on all sides of the issue. Asante's counter plan started to take root. Those gathered at the Canyon Ranch outpost only totaled thirty-three, but they were most of the leaders of the individual factions of The Wave from around the country. Asante requested their presence twelve hours after the initial Farraday interview. She knew if they worked collaboratively they would have a shot for using Farraday's initiative against The Sephiren. Asante believed that if they could demonstrate that The Wave wasn't a cult or terrorists by appealing to the good in people they could eventually illustrate who has been the real threat.

In the interim, members of The Wave, minus the leaders at Canyon Ranch, would willingly go into custody. The plan was that Chelo would lead the group that had been detained from the inside. Asante hoped that her connection to Chelo could be utilized to establish a viable rescue for J.StaRR and the others. The only problem now was time. They didn't have any indication of how much time J.StaRR, Chelo and the others actually had. It had been seventy-two hours since Chelo turned himself in and Asante had not been able to communicate with him. Nyrraw grew impatient and Asante knew they must act fast or he would act alone. She needed to come up with a plan B.

"I don't care what he says, I don't think she's ready for this leadership role. He even said that she still doesn't believe that she is The Aurora while we were in Pismo; don't think I didn't catch that. And why won't he decode the journal, by the way? I know he's Michael, all-powerful telepath and all, but I think he's hiding something." Aissa conjectured as she devoured some sushi at the Canyon Ranch cafeteria sitting at a table with Obadias, Nyrraw, and Marie.

"I think you got to let up, Aissa, you're sounding like a jealous little sister who is mad that big sis has come and stole her shine a bit." Obadias prodded.

Aissa feigned pain in her heart, then said, "Not exactly. The only thing I'm mad at is that we are not going to Guantanamo, guns ablaze, and getting my girl out. We don't have time for this Kumbaya Asante, we need the missile-eating, boiling-blood Asante!" Aissa laughed but was very serious.

"I don't usually agree with your hot-head but at this moment my sister is my first concern, so agreed," Nyrraw said plainly.

Marie looked up at the television hanging in the corner and saw the video of Asante from the Carmel incident. She got up from the table and used a remote to turn up the volume. After the video concluded, a press conference was about to start. President-Elect Douglas was standing next to Farraday at a podium.

"Good evening America. I, unfortunately, will inherit a climate where dealing with heinous acts such as these must be my first priority, which is why my first executive order on the evening of my inauguration will be to eliminate this threat. Despite what these radicals are claiming, these terrorists are extremely dangerous and must be eradicated from our society before they spread like cancer through the body of our nation. This executive order will be effective immediately and will be carried out without haste. Though we have most of this group in custody, members like this Dr. Asante Argueta are still in the wind. Dr. Argueta, if you don't turn yourself and the remaining members in, we will begin using any tactics necessary, including torture, against the members that we do have in custody to attain your whereabouts. Their last moments of life will surely be of agony. You have twenty-four hours. That is all." With that, the news briefing was over.

"It seems as though the decision has just been made for us," Marie said as she turned and looked at them still seated at the table.

*   *   *

Chelo woke up in what he assumed was his cell but it looked more like a corporate conference room. Bright LED lights were recessed in the ceiling above. He was seated alone at a long table unrestrained. Could this be Guantanamo? His instincts told him *no*. He pushed his chair away from the table and tested his feet. Whatever they had sedated him with had apparently worn off. The walls were bare, no two-sided mirrors or cameras. Just a room with one door. He thought *why not* and tested the door to check if it was unlocked. To his surprise, he found that it was. The corridor outside led to two doors at each end. He chose the right door. It led to an office overlooking a bullpen of people working at desks. He then heard water running coming from behind another door inside the office. A moment later a slender woman wearing too much make-up and jewelry emerged.

"Oh, how was your nap, darling?" Stretching out her words in an accent that Chelo couldn't place. He stared at her in response.

"The strong silent type, suit yourself. My name is Adele Vanderneiss and I've been tasked with extracting as much information out of that little mind of yours as possible. Do you know what excites me?" She waited for a beat for a response. But was met with silence. "No matter. What excites me about what I just said is the word *possible*. What limits may we push to get all that we need? Though the Quantum computer has given us much of what we desire, I won't miss out on the realm of possibility when it comes to exploring the details of your mind."

Quantum computer? That's how they found The Wave headquarters, they are toying with us, this has all been a trap, I must warn Asante, Chelo thought.

"Though I cannot read your mind I can imagine your little cognitive wheels turning. Yes, your demise is imminent and no, you can't save her. You should turn your focus to comply in order to minimize the pain which your resistance will inevitably cause."

Chelo tried to dismiss his building fear and connect to the present moment; it was the only way a solution to the quandary he was in could arise. However, as he did, it was like someone was scrambling his focus. He couldn't be present, he couldn't connect to himself much less anyone else or thing. The more he tried, the more distracted and fearful he became.

"What did you do to me?" He said as he lost his footing more from the panic running through his body than anything else.

"Just a little cocktail with a state of the art neural inhibitor. Don't worry it's temporary, but by the time it wears off this will all be over."

Chelo sat down under the weight of the information he had just been given.

*　　*　　*

Asante's building confidence had dwindled to uncertainty by the time she heard of Douglas' mandate. She was now sure she had made the wrong call in surrendering the majority of The Wave. She probably just cost them all of their lives, including Chelo, at which the thought of, rocked her to her core. *We have always been and will be.* She thought of his words as water filled her eyes and pain and regret filled her heart. What had she done?

"May I sit next to you?"

Startled a bit, she looked up to find Michael. She hadn't heard him enter the meditation room where she sat. She nodded as she wiped away her tears and collected herself.

"Have to say, I'm not feeling it," Asante said right away.

"Why, because you fell into a trap?"

"Yes. I'm a failure and because of it, people I love are going to die. People that make the world better because they are in it. People that were truly the hope for humankind and I'm responsible...I can't, I can't..." Asante began to weep.

Michael was silent while he rubbed her back. He then wiped her tears and pushed her hair out of her face. He abruptly grabbed her chin and held her face close to his own and stared into her eyes.

"Now that you've got it out, get over it. This isn't your first mistake or your last but it can be one that you learn and grow from. When it seems you can't make a move, be still and go inside yourself. There will lie your answers, there will be your truth, and there will be your greatest power. He needs you, go to him with your greatest strength, your love," with this, Michael got up and left the room.

*   *   *

Chelo had been escorted from the office overlooking the bullpen of workers, back down the corridor to the door he originally chose not to go through. In the room was a machine that looked like it was used for CAT scans. There was a table in which he was instructed to lay upon and a larger machine that the table entered into once he did. He was told to relax and to watch and listen for the audiovisual prompts. He knew that they had his mind, but he knew Asante had his heart and that their souls were connected. He started to feel heat in his head and body which he suspected came from the machine. Although, his body was experiencing pain he knew there was a part of him that only knew love. He sought after it amidst the abyss of agony. He took a deep breath and more air than he could naturally take in filled his lungs. The air seemed to fill and surround his whole being. A feeling of peace and love enveloped his body. Asante. He didn't know how, but he could feel her, almost smell her in the air that was lifting him off of the table.

The technicians that had brought him into the room rushed in and fought against the mini-whirlwind that engulfed him. After a few moments battling the force of the air encircling his body, they finally reached him and pulled him out of the machine, which had malfunctioned and was now smoking. As they did, the winds stopped and all was still. But it was too late. Though it had only been a few moments of connection between he and Asante, the love that flowed in the air that rushed through and around his body was so powerful that it healed him at that moment. His mind was no longer fragmented thoughts and images that he couldn't control but sharp focus and connection had returned. He smiled to himself and thought, *will always be*, as he was led out of the room.

Asante opened her eyes. She wasn't sure what she had just experienced. She had sought to find Chelo with her heart instead of her mind as her father had suggested. The air had begun to rush in her ears, but this time instead of it feeling like it was separate from herself and she was encountering it, she allowed her whole self to become a part of it, so that her whole being was one with it. It was in that space that she was reunited with her love, that she could sense Quantum, the weapon they had been using against The Wave, and that she finally understood that she is The Aurora but she is never alone.

Chapter 22 The War
Part 2

Emily Argueta was fourteen years old and alone. She knew that she was lost on the path she had chosen. Her perfect family would never understand the torment in which she experienced in loving him. He was her physics teacher at Babylon High School. He was brilliant, he had noticed her wit on the first day of school.

"Newtonian versus Quantum?" He asked the class with his piercing blue eyes behind his tortoiseshell glasses. Ezra Farraday's reputation as a thought-provoking hard-ass teacher had preceded him, but Emily was no slouch. She raised her hand but waited until their eyes met to begin speaking.

"A bike versus space travel. They both have their purpose, dependent upon what you are aiming to experience along your journey. I personally want to see the stars, but I also can appreciate the beauty of a flower on my way to school." She said without a hint of intimidation or doubt as she stared into his eyes.

He smirked more to himself, "A clever analogy, Miss..."

"Argueta." She said coolly. Their question and response dance began that day and would continue all year. Emily was way ahead of grade level and would only turn thirteen at the end of her freshman year where she held a 4.0 in all of her Advanced Placement classes. Despite himself and better judgment, Ezra Farraday was struck by her brilliance and beauty. Her olive reddish skin was radiant juxtapose her natural strawberry blonde hair. She was the perfect blend of her mixed Anglo and Latin heritage. By the end of the year, their classroom banter grew into an after class, in-depth discussion, and study.

They agreed to keep each other abreast of any news articles on physics over the summer. But their extracurricular affair began after their first meeting once the school year had concluded. By the time they had got to the door of the hotel room that night they were all over each other, kissing deeply and exploring the feel of each other's bodies which they had longed to touch for so many months. The next morning Emily woke up next to the man she hoped to spend the rest of her life with. The room service and half-empty glasses of wine adorned the room--evidence of the epic night they just had. Emily was in love and Ezra Farraday finally belonged to her. He was the only one who really understood her. He saw all of her being and not just the parts that suited him. She adoringly ran her fingers through his hair while he slept. She stared at him for a few moments, then got up to use the bathroom and freshen up. On her way there she nearly tripped over his pants. She picked them up and his wallet fell out and laid open on the floor. Emily bent down to pick it up and her breath caught in her chest as she stared down at a picture of Farraday with what appeared to be his family in his wallet. Farraday looked straight ahead while in his arms was a short-haired blonde woman who looked up at him with a baby in her arms of no more than three to four months of age. Emily pulled the picture out of the wallet and turned it over: *5.26.84, Home Sweet Home.* Last Month. She then looked at the address listed on his license in the opposite flap. The room around her started to spin. A moment later Emily fainted.

*   *   *

"So what is a quantum computer exactly, I could sense some of its properties, but how does it work?" Asante asked Brad in the middle of their discussion about what she had experienced with Chelo. She had sought out Brad as she remembered his propensity to understand how things work from when they were first introduced.

"The easiest way to explain it is that standard computers process information in a series of zeros and ones. Well, instead of computing linearly, in a quantum computer the zeros and ones are in superposition of one another so the relationship is exponential. The filter or range it's encoded with selects the most probable answer with the least amount of error considering a quantum amount of possibility. Which is far more possibility than standard computers can even factor," Brad stated as a matter of fact.

"That's how The Sephiren found The Wave headquarters...That means they already know where we are, so why are they pretending not to?" Asante asked, working through her thoughts and questions out loud.

"The long game," Brad answered after a moment of reflection. "The Sephiren could ask their quantum computer our location but that doesn't guarantee what they want. That's probably what they did the last time and none of us were captured."

"You are right, they are drawing us out not only to destroy us but to eradicate the possibility of the truth we carry from ever spreading. They want to have a war to end it all." Asante continued his train of thought.

"Correction, she wants a war to end it all and wants to use The Wave as the scapegoat for the greatest attack against humankind from which true consciousness will never return," Michael claimed as he entered the conference room at Canyon Ranch.

"How do we even combat something of that magnitude?" Asante asked, overwhelmed with the thought of the world without hope.

"We beat her at her own game. Wasn't that the plan before we knew she was using Quantum against us? The knowledge of Quantum should inform the way we move but not deter us from our aim. She wants a war, let's give her one," Michael said with fire in his eyes.

*   *   *

The note she found by the bed when Emily came to, said it all: *As you've assessed, my life is a bit more complicated than I've expressed. You are a great girl and I thank you for being there for me during a difficult time. I hope for you all the success the universe has to offer. I will not be returning to Babylon High School in the fall, but you will do great things in your life, please know that I know that, Sincerely, Ezra.*

The moments before she passed out flooded her mind's eye. Loss turned into fear, fear into pain, and pain into a rage that Emily didn't know was possible. She steadied her shaking hands as she took a pad and pen out of the nightstand next to the bed. She began to write down the address she had seen on his driver's license before she passed out.

Emily went home to a house that didn't know she was gone.

"Hey Ems," her brother Michael greeted her as she entered the front door. "Off to baseball, then evening surf, see you later, huh?" He said as he rushed out the door, carrying too much equipment for one person to handle.

She went straight up the stairs to her room. Once she closed and locked her door, she went directly to her dresser and pulled out the bottom drawer. She reached behind it and pulled out a book entitled "Chaos Magick," she had been studying secretly since her family had all but abandoned her when she tried manipulating their precious *Wave* to teach some brats at her school a lesson.

She had manipulated the water in the school swimming pool so that the swim team including her foes, Kiley and Kennedy, couldn't breach the water's surface. She stood above them laughing while they all panicked grasping for air under the surface of the water. Of course superhero Michael intervened before anyone drowned.

"I was just scaring them," Emily offered up as a defense. But her mother and father saw it entirely different.

"This is not what we are about, Emily. We are here to help humankind evolve; not to evoke fear!" Her mother's sheer disappointment was written all over her face.

"Take a page from your brother. In the interim, we are ending your training until you demonstrate some real compassion," her father added.

She had been seeking a belief system that embodied her natural proclivities. She found answers in *Chaos Magick*. She could use what she had learned about the connection to the physical universe through The Wave and apply it without repercussion using the freedom that Chaos Magick provided. She threw the book, clothes, and some money she had saved into a backpack.

"Are you ok, Emily?" Her mother said as she knocked on the other side of her bedroom door.

"I'm fine," Emily answered without emotion, though her eyes were full of tears.

"I know you're hurting. I just wanted to let you know I'm here when you want to talk," her mother responded.

"I know, Mom, thanks," Emily said as she reached for a shoebox in the back of her closet. She opened it to find the sigil she had created for her intentions for her and Ezra. She wrapped it in a t-shirt and put it in the backpack. Emily took one more look around as she opened the window to her bedroom and climbed out onto the lattice. Once she reached the ground she calmly began to walk toward Ezra's house.

*   *   *

The deadline that Douglas and Farraday stipulated in their last news conference for the remaining Wave members to turn themselves in was fast approaching. Chelo had escaped Quanta fairly easily after feigning to cooperate with Vanderneiss' experiments while he tried to glean information from and hack into their quantum computer. However, either the security protocols on the machine itself were too extensive or someone had already done what he was attempting and was already connected to the computer from a quantum electrodynamic standpoint. He figured it was the latter and decided to escape before he was discovered.

He now sat in a circle with the other leaders of The Wave poised to launch their counter-attack on The Sephiren. Though his surrender gave them insight as it relates to the quantum computer, they were no closer in determining where J.StaRR and the other members were being held or if they were even still alive. Meanwhile, the general public continued to divide on the question that the existence of The Wave asked: *Are we happy with the way things are or are we willing to be open to something potentially better?* For the first time since the last real shift in human history after the Civil Rights movement, people were actually asking questions of their conscience.

Asante and Michael had decided to take advantage of this reprieve in the clutter of distraction in the human psyche and speak directly to the heart of man. The remaining leaders of The Wave had created a circle of protective energy around Michael and Asante while Michael interrupted all live television networks. Then he used his eyes as a camera and began to broadcast Asante as she spoke to the world.

"Good evening, we are communicating with you via the same means that The Sephiren demonstrated some of our natural abilities. When I say, *our,* I mean specifically every human being that occupies this planet. When I say, *The Sephiren,* I mean the organized effort that has been keeping this knowledge a secret contained amongst a few. The Wave are the few that have been maintaining this knowledge pretty much since the dawn of humanity. Just like we've always been, so has The Sephiren. The difference now is that for the first time in human history instead of political or social shifts that we have been a part of creating--the effects of our knowledge has been spreading through the consciousness of man. And The Sephiren are scared. Frightened that their hold on humanity is slipping through their grasps. Let's do an experiment together to provide evidence for the truth in which I speak.

"Everyone who can see and or hear me, let's meditate or even focus on the location of the four forty-four members of The Wave that surrendered themselves. The Sephiren and government officials have said that they are being held at Guantanamo Bay, let's see if that's even true. I will begin a guided meditation in a moment, through this meditation the location of The Wave members should become a clear mental picture behind your closed eyes. Let's start by taking three deep clearing breaths.

Inhale truth, freedom, and awareness. Exhale fear, pain, and anxiety." Asante closed her eyes and began to breathe.

"Now, think of those being held as yourself, your mothers, brothers, sisters or children. Identify your love for yourself and your loved ones. Now see where they are, what does it look like, smell like? Is it cold or hot? What is it called?"

At that moment, everyone in the room and hundreds of thousands across the world saw in their mind's eye the location of the four forty-four. *Farraday Laboratories and Research* read the sign on the building.

"Now that we know where they are, what are we going to do about it?" Asante looked deeply into Michael's eyes. "Until we meet again, ride The Wave, the truth is inside you."

Michael closed his eyes and severed the connection.

"Missile fired. Bet she didn't see that coming!"

T.O.R.N.

*   *   *

Waiting had never been Emily's area of expertise. However, that is exactly what she had been doing for the past two days. She had watched the Farraday's lead their happy life from the bushes in their backyard. They had been packing and loading a moving truck parked in their driveway. She surmised that they were leaving soon from how full the truck was getting and how empty the house seemed. Last night she found shelter in their backyard shed while she fantasized about what was going on inside the house. But instead of his happy wife at the helm of their beautiful world, Emily saw herself with the short blonde haircut and baby in tow.

As the morning light crept into the sky, she knew that the next opportunity for her to enter the house without Ezra there was approaching. He soon would leave for pastries, newspaper, and coffee, probably for the last time before they departed. It would be now or lose her love forever.

"Ok see you in a bit," Ezra said as he exited the side kitchen door.

Emily waited until she heard the engine of his car dissipate as he drove down the street and away from the house. She entered through the same unlocked side kitchen door. Ezra's wife was rummaging through the refrigerator with her back to Emily as she entered the kitchen. The baby was in a high chair to Emily's left. When Ezra's wife closed the refrigerator and turned around to face her child, she dropped the glass bowl of rice cereal and the milk that was in her hands at the terrifying sight that greeted her.

Emily stood behind the baby with the pointed edge of her sigil at the baby's throat.

"I'll do anything, there's money in my purse, just please don't hurt Remy. Please," She was shaking with fear as tears ran down her face. How could Ezra love someone so weak, so powerless? But she was beautiful. She only looked a few years older than herself now that Emily could take in the countenance of her whole face instead of her profile from the picture.

Never taking her eyes off his wife, Emily took the baby out of the high chair with one arm and held the sigil to his neck with the other.

126

"Open the bag, and take out the chalk, candle, and matches." Emily nodded toward her backpack which she had placed on the kitchen table between them.

Ezra's wife did so and carefully placed the items on the table.

"Light the candle, then take the chalk and draw the shape of this on the ground. Don't deviate or mess up in anyway or else," Emily held the sigil out slightly away from the baby so that Ezra's wife could get a good look at it. She did as she was instructed.

"Please just let me hold him," She pleaded.

"Stand in the middle of the shape you drew on the floor and I will," Emily responded, never taking her eyes off of her. Once again Ezra's wife did as she was told. Emily walked in a circle around the drawing of the Sigil in the floor and Ezra's wife and began to repeat her intentions for herself and Ezra.

His wife began to scream for her baby, Emily spoke faster and louder as she encircled her, drawing closer and closer. Finally, Emily embraced her with the baby as Ezra's wife grasped the infant tightly. But a moment later surprise and pain loosened her grip as her knees buckled beneath her and she stumbled to the ground still holding the baby. She saw drops of her own blood dripping from the sigil in Emily's hand as she stood above her.

"He's mine. And now that I've imprinted your essence onto this sigil, which binds us, he'll love me the way he loves you! Don't worry I'll take good care of Remy!" Emily said as she bent down to take the infant from her arms.

As she did, Ezra's wife grabbed her shirt and pulled Emily close enough for her to whisper in her ear and said, "My brother will never love you!" Emily pulled back to look at her in confusion, but it was too late, her eyes stared blankly with death. Remy began to cry.

Brother? No, this was his wife and child. No, no, no, no. Emily scanned the kitchen and saw a purse hanging on the back of a chair. She emptied the contents on the table. Emily found her wallet and found the same picture she had found in Ezra's wallet. She slowly turned over the picture to read: *Best brother and uncle ever. 5.26.84.* Her heart began to race as she heard the engine of Ezra's car pull into the driveway. He'll never love me. He'll never forgive me. She could hear his footsteps on the gravel in the driveway.

Emily grabbed her backpack and ran out the front door. Just as she reached the sidewalk, she heard him call out in agony.

"No, no, baby sis! No, no, help, help!" He wailed as she began to run down the street.

*   *   *

It had been a year since that day. A year of mindless wandering; drugging and numbing out the pain that haunted her daily as Ezra's cries echoed in Emily's mind. She knew she was lost on the path she had chosen, but she didn't want to be found. She didn't want forgiveness, restoration, or love. She only wanted what had escaped her, control. If she had control none of this would have happened. Emily would have been the happy Mrs. Ezra Farraday, but she was lost forever. Emily decided *Mrs. Ezra Farraday* was a victim of circumstance and would never be. *Dr. Emily Farraday* would prevail. She will have control like no other. She was determined to find her within herself and she vowed that once she did, she would never let her or the control she wields go.

The Sephiren was the only answer, they were the only ones with the true power to facilitate the control she desired. Emily's family had taught her about the destructive power The Sephiren had used against humanity. It was that power that she would serve and in return, the world would be under her control.

Chapter 23
The War
Part 3

Brennan knew that The Sephiren had been able to track him before Asante saved him. He assumed that they had discarded him as no longer useful. Or, somehow, when Asante saved his life, the process left the method in which they had been tracking him inoperable. Because they had left him alone since the helicopter exploded. He hadn't tried to make contact with Asante either in case the truth of the situation was that The Sephiren were waiting for him to do so that they could orchestrate another trap for her.

By the time he hiked out of the Santa Lucia Mountains he was determined to be reunited with her—if she would have him—and do whatever was in his power to destroy The Sephiren. He always had an intuition that his relationship with The Sephiren might end in turmoil which is why he worked so hard to prove himself valuable, despite his inability to entrain the world around him.

However, the most incredible thing happened while he hiked. For the first time in his life, he was able to be present and connect to the elements around him. It was beautiful and he was baffled by his previous notions of exploiting this ability and understood that it was a harmonious relationship between himself and the universe. That it is the most synergetic and efficient way of existing. He wasn't sure about what he was specifically aligned to yet, but he knew he could integrate now and wanted to be a part of spreading the truth. After he reached his off-the-grid safe house in the rural area of Montgomery Township, New Jersey, a little less than a week later, he had been enthralled with the unfolding of that truth on a national and global scale.

The war for humanity had begun and both sides were playing to win. The last counter-attack from Asante and The Wave this morning when they launched a worldwide meditation to glean the location of the four forty-four set the world ablaze with a thirst for more. The truth spread because the experience couldn't be denied. People's understanding of the mass meditation was without fear which caused them to immediately recognize the freedom that had been absent from their lives. People who were scared of The Wave only moments before were now questioning the way things had been and were eager to explore the possibilities of what The Wave claimed to be true. The fabric of the deception pulled over man's eyes was torn and light was shining in on a new reality.

By dusk, the Dow had slipped to a record-breaking low. Walk-outs at places of work and education had been widespread, protests, and riots broke out calling for the immediate release of the four forty-four all over the world. The Sephiren had been silent all day.

Brennan decided to take a breath and meditate. He looked at the clock on his wall five fifty-five pm. He closed his eyes and set his intention to be ready. He didn't know when, he didn't know how, but he knew he would be prepared and that he'd never fail her again.

There was no way to tell if their broadcast had delayed the demise of J.StaRR and the four forty-four or sped up Farraday's intention for the group. However, the broadcast did change the playing field. After identifying herself as Asante Argueta to the operator at Atlantic Aviation, she was able to charter a plane within minutes for them to get to Mac Arthur Airport on Long Island, only fifteen minutes away from Farraday Research and Laboratories.

After booking the trip for all thirty-three of them the operator surprisingly ended the call with "Go get them, ride The Wave, Asante." Which surprised her but also left Asante pontificating the impact of their broadcast.

The four-hour flight gave her and the others time to discuss it. She knew the move would cause discord on the grid but she did not anticipate the response to be as immediate as it appeared to be manifesting.

"The world is actually waking up before our eyes! I can feel the shift energetically already!" Marie exclaimed as she checked Instagram mid-flight.

"I hope so, but I can't help but feel like it's all happening too fast for some reason? Like we're not seeing something, you know what I mean?" Asante asked turning to Michael.

"Rightly so, you are smart to never underestimate your aunt, but it was the best choice for us to make with the options she left us with and we now have her on the defense," Michael responded.

"Besides, now with all the people protesting at the lab, she can't hurt them because she's publicly aligned herself with the government, which the masses are still under this belief that they answer to the people. She'd risk an all-out anarchy at least in this country if she made that move," Marie added.

"Unless that is what she wants, and in the case that she's hurt Joi, she's going to get it and a whole lot more," Nyrraw finished the conversation with this statement and gave them all more to contemplate for the rest of the trip.

But nothing they thought of prepared them for what greeted them when they arrived at Farraday Research and Laboratories a few hours later that night.

About a mile outside of the facility is where they first saw them. People. Thousands and thousands of protestors lined the streets. Signs that read "Freedom now 4 the 444" and "Free the 444" were everywhere. Asante rolled down her window to hear people chanting, "We are The Wave, no more Sephiren, we are The Wave."

Asante didn't know if it was the number of people or the possibility of what Farraday might do, but the scene was unsettling to her nerves and she could feel fear spread through her body like the cold tranquilizer The Sephiren had first used on her back at The Fairchild Estate. She sat paralyzed, glued to her seat for a moment, when Chelo who sat next to her, grabbed her hand.

He looked into her eyes and said, "I know you're The Aurora, you know it, now they do. There's nothing to fear," as the words left his lips, sensation returned to her body, but something was coming, she could feel it.

*   *   *

When Brennan woke up, sweat poured down his face to his soaked white t-shirt. He had laid down after his meditation for a brief nap and his dreams were flooded with terrifying premonitions. He was outside of the Farraday Research Building surrounded by thousands of protestors when he locked eyes with Asante who was getting out of an SUV, but when he looked at her his point of view changed from being able to see her directly in front of him, to watching himself lock eyes with her, as if outside of himself. To watching a thousand versions of himself lock eyes with her as if he were looking at the scene through a funny mirror at a carnival. Then it seemed as though fire rained down from the sky all around them while the earth shook beneath their feet. He went to protect Asante from danger by pulling her closer to himself. His point of view changed again and now he could see Asante directly in front of himself once more, but he could feel the weight of water all around them. They were suddenly under water. Asante smiled at him then floated to the surface above. He tried to follow her but found he couldn't move. The sensation of not being able to breathe filled his lungs and body and just when he knew he was approaching his last moment of life, he woke up.

He got out of the bed and begun to pack a bag, he knew what he must do.

*   *   *

The caravan of SUVs they traveled in toward Farraday Research and Laboratories stopped about a thousand feet from the front gate of the facility because they could get no closer. The depth of the crowd was too great as protestors had completely flooded the streets. Asante looked at Chelo one more time before getting out of the black twenty-eighteen Suburban, his eyes always gave her confidence. But the next set of eyes that she met as her feet hit the ground shook her.

Brennan.

They stood there in silence for a moment while all the noise of the protests faded in their connection. Chelo reintroduced the sound in the scene when he approached Asante's side and grabbed her hand.

"Are you ok?" He said and then realized who she was staring at in the crowd. Brennan took two steps forward and finally took his gaze off Asante and held out his hand to introduce himself to Chelo.

"Dr. Brennan Valdis," he offered.

Chelo wasn't having it, immediately sensing the connection between the two of them.

"Yeah, ok," Chelo said, giving him a once over and completely ignoring his hand. He grabbed Asante's arm and began to usher her away with their backs toward Valdis.

After a few steps, Asante stopped and said, "Wait he's here to help."

Chelo looked at her as if she had two heads and said, "Actually, he's here for you."

By this time Aissa, Marie, Obadias, Nyrraw, Brad, Michael and the others surrounded them.

"If you don't trust him, scan him," Michael interjected.

Chelo stepped squarely in front of Brennan who stepped forward though still apprehensive about what might be found.

"Before you do, know that I'm aware there may be a surveillance device in my body, but it's not of my own volition. I am no longer a part of The Sephiren and I am here for her, but more importantly, I'm here to help."

Chelo took in the information without response and began the scan. Within moments he said, "You have an ocular implant that has the ability to feed live or record."

"What!" Everyone gasped in disbelief.

"They most likely developed the technology using the information they gathered during my experiments at Sing Sing," Michael offered.

"Yes, that makes sense. The tech emulates what you are able to do while entrained." Brad concluded.

"Is it active?" Asante asked.

"Not now, but it's still connected, but you did just prove that you could turn out to be useful. I'll monitor the device and see if there's a way to hack it when it does go live and get into the computer it's connected to. Hopefully, they've networked it to Quantum, and I can find a backdoor route to access it." Chelo told the group.

Their small group had been so engrossed in their conversation that they hadn't noticed when Asante was recognized by one of the protestors. A hush spread through the crowd as thousands of eyes and phones were all on her.

The gate to the facility began to open slowly. The crowd split apart creating a path for Asante and the others to move forward toward the opening gate. As they walked through the doors of the facility opened and J.StaRR came staggering out.

Nyrraw and Aissa ran toward her immediately. By the time they reached her, she was on the ground. The Misfitz and the rest of the Four-forty-four began streaming out of the building. The protestors erupted in cheers and applause. Nyrraw grabbed his sister in his arms pushing her lavender braids out of her face.

She seemed like she was barely conscious when she opened her eyes briefly and managed, "They did something to me, I can't control it," As the words left her mouth a huge jolt shook the ground. A moment later the ground beneath them shook so violently that a huge crack split directly under the Farraday Research Building and through the center of the crowd. Panic and terror seized the moment. Some fell into the gaping and spreading hole in the earth; people ran in every direction. Fires erupted from the explosions that started in the building as it was torn apart. The ground continued to shake.

Nyrraw and Aissa carried J.StaRR to the others who were running toward them.

"They did something to trigger her and she can't control it. I think she's shifting the Ramapo Fault line. If we don't stop it this whole island and half the eastern seaboard will be submerged in water in moments."

"What if I try and disrupt the frequency and attempt to stop the plates from moving?" Aissa asked.

"Theoretically it might work, it's worth a shot," Brad answered.

Aissa closed her eyes. "It's too strong, I can't locate the point in which she's entrained, it's almost as if it's not coming from her," Aissa opened her eyes.

"It's not, it's Douglas, I remember from the police station. The way he moved with the ground as it shook he must be aligned with the tectonic plates as well." Asante realized.

"Oh, my God! They are going to kill us all!" Aissa exclaimed.

The ground then moved in a way that didn't seem possible. As if it were as malleable as water. Then after one more large bolt, everything was still. They all looked around taking in the devastation. It was as if they had entered a war zone. Everything was on fire, bodies strewn about the street, the injured looked lost, barely holding onto life.

Water filled Asante's eyes, but before the emotion could really engulf her, the blowing in her ears began. All the hairs on her body stood up at once. It was as if a gust of wind blew past her. The force of which made her stumble a bit. She looked around and no one else seemed to be aware of what she was experiencing. She turned eastbound and the intensity in which the wind blew increased.

"Something is coming," she whispered into the night.

She looked up at the full moon in the sky and noticed a swarm of seagulls flying inland. The blowing was so intense that it seemed to lift her feet off the ground. She looked down to find that she was actually levitating. It hit her. She knew what was coming.

She turned and screamed, "Tsunami, run!"

They all looked up and at first saw nothing in the sky, but after a moment the stars in the distance began to disappear and a shimmering black surface was reflected in the moonlight. A massive wall of water at least five hundred feet high was rushing toward them all as far as the eye could see.

"We'll never outrun it in time," Aissa said with fear all over her face.

"Believe. Run little sister, save as many as you can!" Asante said back assertively.

They locked eyes for a moment, not knowing if they would ever see each other again, embraced and Aissa left her with, "You got it, sissy, I know you're in charge!" She turned with the others and started to move as they screamed to the survivors, "Run, Run, Tsunami, Run!"

Asante turned to face the oncoming tsunami and found Chelo was at her side, "You didn't think I'd let you face this alone?"

Now the emotion that was building in her flooded down her face.

"I know, but you have to; like you said, I am The Aurora. I was created for this moment. I feel it in every part of myself. I'm no longer afraid. I'll never be alone again. We've always been and we always will be. But right now they need you," Asante said pointing to the people amidst the destruction.

"But I need you."

Asante put her finger over his mouth, then kissed him and said, "Believe."

He looked at her one last time and ran into the night. Brennan standing a few feet away heard it all and realized the full meaning of his premonition as the sensation of not being able to breathe returned to his body. She wouldn't have him and part of him died in that moment. But in looking around he found purpose and a new part of his heart began to beat. He ran into the darkness determined to be the light.

The tsunami was so close that Asante could hear the rushing water drawing close to her. All that she had experienced up until this moment played in her mind's eye. However, the movie that played was flashing images in reverse as if she was going backward in time. Before she knew it she was in her childhood bedroom in Oakland with her sister and mother.

Stella was saying, "One day you'll need to be braver and stronger than you've ever been, but have also always been, and you'll need to remember this song to do so. So sing this song with Mommy, so that you'll never forget who you are, who you've been, and who you will always be."

Asante opened her eyes as the wave was upon her, held up her hands and began to sing, "I am ready for the day, I am kind, I am brave. I'm exactly what I say, not tomorrow but today! I am ready for today, night is gone, I'm awake. There is no time anyway, let's have fun and create. Don't delay, ride the waves, I am ready for the day. I am ready for the day, I am ready for the day." With every stanza, she felt herself become one with the ocean. With its energy, with its life, she could feel herself connect on a molecular level. As the crest of the wave was towering over her head she prevented it from moving any further--suspended in mid-air. The light of the moon shone through the water. At first, Asante could see sea life in the deep, but after a moment a light in the dark water flickered in the distance. As she focused on it she could make out one form that became several as they seemingly came toward her. It was Stella in front and what seemed like generations of women behind her. The last figure had a face that seemed so familiar, it looked like herself, only older with long silver-gray hair in two braids on the sides of her head. She smiled at Asante, then took a deep breath and blew it out. As she did--every woman before her seemed as though they caught the breath and blew it out into the being of the woman in front of them until the chain of breath reached Stella who took one last breath and blew it out. As she did, the blowing in Asante's ears began again and rushed through her being out through her fingertips into the direction of The Wave. As if being controlled by the energy emanating from Asante, the wave of the tsunami changed orientation and began to recede in the other direction.

A few moments later the moon became visible again as the water disappeared. When the sight of the water was far enough in the distance on the horizon, Asante took a breath and said "Roselyn," as she lost consciousness and collapsed.

Chapter 24
Escape

"We warned you that they were terrorists, we demonstrated proof of their abilities, yet you called for their release as if we're not here to protect the best interest of this great nation and the global community. And in striving to be transparent and for the people, against our better judgment, we released the four forty-four to demonstrate a spirit of cooperation and understanding. However, within moments of their release, The Wave launched the single greatest attack on American soil this nation has ever seen. From Maine to North Carolina the Eastern Seaboard was completely decimated by the earthquake and tsunami they caused. Only sparing New York to save their own wretched souls. A natural disaster orchestrated by their manipulation? What reign of terror will be next? Millions of Americans lost not only their lives last night, but those that survived, their security in the American Dream. How can we afford to lose anymore? Make no mistake this was an act of war. We must respond in kind now! I'm asking for a special session of Congress to be called in order to enact a Declaration of War against this group and those that support them. We must stand together on this issue, this isn't a partisan problem, but a national and global one. Again, The Wave is the threat that must be stopped by any means necessary. Be vigilant America, our way of life depends on it. God bless you and God bless the United States of America." Douglas looked directly into the camera for several moments before leaving the podium.

As he left the press room, the first set of eyes that met him were of Emily Farraday.

"You know there is no precedence for this?" Douglas glared at her.

"Have you forgotten about the Civil War?" Emily said with a smirk that she couldn't help.

"I doubt the American people and the rest of the world will see it that way after the stunt the Argueta girl pulled." Douglas shot back.

"You overestimate their attention. The only thing they will remember is what fits most easily into the paradigm The Sephiren has established. We determine the truth, and we will annihilate any doubt that The Wave has sprouted," Emily responded confidently.

"You may have convinced The Counsel to vote *yes* on the earthquake I caused this time, but this is not the way of The Sephiren. We've always been able to have a firm hand in the fate of humanity by disabling it of its greatest asset; the highest self. But your game with your family has made that asset accessible. You are pushing mankind to make a choice, one in which its never even been aware of; bound by the security of what he's known or freedom in the abyss of the unknown. For your sake, I hope they choose wisely." Douglas spat as he turned abruptly and walked away from Farraday. His threat sinking into the pit of her stomach.

*   *   *

The light that tore through the fabric of deception over mankind had gone out. And a gaping black hole was left in its stead. The newfound hope for the possibility of what *could be* was a distant memory in the wake of the destruction the earthquake and tsunami caused. The world needed healing but so did Asante. She hadn't opened her eyes since she collapsed three days earlier and her life seemed to be slipping away from her as her pulse had become fainter over the last twelve hours. All the surviving members of The Wave had made it to Manhattan and had set up a make-shift headquarters in one of the last buildings that remained standing, The New York City Public Library.

Aissa, Michael, Nyrraw, Chelo, Obadias, Marie, J.StaRR, Brad, and Massah had encircled her nearly lifeless body when they arrived and did everything within their power to bring her back. From prayer and meditation to creating a bridge for her consciousness to travel back from the formless to form. But they couldn't reach her. Their hope began to fade into their broken hearts by the early morning of the fourth day. The legislation for the Declaration of War against them passed unanimously the night before. The Sephiren would soon come for them. They were out of time.

"I don't understand," Aissa cried as she held Asante's limp hand in her own. "You said she was The Aurora. You had us believe it, how can this be happening right now?" She looked up at Michael with a mixture of rage and confusion.

"Maybe we saw what we wanted to see, maybe our own desperation for change saw prophecy where there was only coincidence," Michael said in response searching his mind for answers.

"What the hell does that mean, what was in that journal?"

Water filled Michael's eyes, he took a moment to gather himself, cleared his throat and said, "Your mother and I were both from families that were keepers of The Wave. Through my father's Taino Maroon heritage and your mother's Nigerian and Wappo heritage. However, as we traveled the world and studied older more ancient civilizations from Mesopotamia and Harappan-Indus Valley, Egypt and Kush, Ancient China, and The Mayan people, we found stories that sounded like our own. We found our ancestors, our bloodlines dating back to the inception of man on this earth. We then knew our love wasn't by chance, that the culmination of the new age by The Aurora referred to as 'timeless' would come from us. One tradition spoke of it this way, '*when the timeless one appears, all that came before and all that will ever be, will be as one, the war of yesterday will fade and the paradise of tomorrow will become reality today, through the promise of a love forged before time began*,' but maybe we saw what we wanted to see," He said shaking his head in defeat. All of them looked at him in awe.

After a moment, Aissa asked, "And how did you know it wasn't me?"

Michael looked at Aissa with so much love in his eyes and said, "It's not just what we've seen her do, it's *how*. We've all been taught to be in The Now, to be present and entrain. Yes, some of us have been triggered by heightened states of emotion, pushing us into this reality, but not to entrain with such mastery. It's as if she has alignment with every element of this dimension. How is that possible? Asante healed without knowing how, connected with me when I was still in Sing Sing, again how? Look at what she did to that Sherriff in Carmel, or with the missile from the helicopter, and finally the tsunami, who taught her, where does her mastery of The Now come from? It's because she's somehow timeless, she's connected to the moment as if nothing else exists," Michael said as everyone thought the same unifying thought. She is The Aurora.

They all looked at each other for a moment as the truth of their collective thought lit a spark of hope in the darkness.

"So what do we do?" Aissa asked

"The only thing we have left; believe!" Answered Marie.

* * *

"We have confirmed the location Quantum provided this morning. All the remaining members of The Wave, including the Argueta family, are at the New York Public Library. We have an authorized airstrike waiting for your go," Fairchild stated as he entered into Farraday's office at CIA headquarters in Langley, Virginia.

"There is no room for error. There can be no escape. An aerial attack won't ensure that. We can use it as a facade for the American people after we have confirmed their destruction. Send in The Sephiren Assassins that Carmichael had been training on the ground first, take them out, then destroy the building from the air." Emily said coldly.

"The assassins are bloodthirsty mercenaries that have been experimented on to the point that they are barely human and can't be controlled. They will kill anyone in their path, there are still droves of innocent people fighting for their lives waiting to be rescued on that island. It's not safe, for the survivors, to unleash them," Fairchild explained.

"Fuck 'em, casualties of war," Emily said and gave Fairchild a look that scared him to his core.

In response, he only could muster, "Yes ma'am, right away. I'll get them assembled immediately."

* * *

Brennan had been making himself useful. His training as a trauma surgeon proved to be invaluable for the survivors in the hours after the attack. He, like millions of other survivors, had made their way to Manhattan to be reunited with family and be connected with FEMA until transportation out of the area could be established. The encampment for FEMA was in front of the New York Public

141

Library. As he looked around the medical area of the large tent, he saw humanity at its best. And yet, without any of the possessions—only a few hours earlier—they so desperately needed. Humankind was set free and the best of them were illustrated in the faces of the survivors. Human citizen helping human citizen without fear, prejudice, or distraction. Love appeared. Tears filled his eyes, and blurred red lines flooded his vision. He wiped his tears and the red lines became clear beams of red light. They were aimed, what at first glance looked like random people, but as Brennan followed each beam of light, they were all aimed at people of authority or security under the tent.

He shouted, "Move!" As loud as he could but the sound of gunfire swallowed up his voice.

Everyone that was able to—scattered in every direction. Brennan ran toward the perimeter of the tent. Dressed in all black were men with artillery that Brennan had never seen. The Sephiren, he thought. He didn't know what he could entrain with yet, but he knew if the people around him had a chance of surviving it was dependent on his ability to disarm at least one of these men to get a weapon. He singularly focused on that intention as he ran toward one of the assassins.

As he did, he was able to see the trajectory of the bullets in his mind's eye and dodge impact accordingly. In moments Brennan was face-to-face with one of them in hand-to-hand combat. It lasted only seconds because he could, again, see where the assassin would strike before impact. The result was Brennan was one step ahead of him. He disarmed and knocked the assassin unconscious in almost one motion. Brennan then began to hunt the assassins in the midst of all the chaos.

* * *

Young Chase came running into the room where they still sat encircled around Asante.

"They're here. The Sephiren are here. But they have not breached the building. Instead, they are in the street attacking survivors!"

"We have to help them." Marie was overwhelmed with emotion.

"We can't leave Asante, we have to protect her," Chelo declared.

"We'll stay here. Chase take everyone else and go save as many as you can, now!" Yelled Aissa.

They all looked at each other around the circle in silent agreement that they'd give their last breath to save Asante.

As they breathed in this collective agreement, Brad was hit with inspiration. "I have an idea. We may be able to get out of here. Is Brennan outside?"

Michael, Marie, and Chelo simultaneously answered "Yes."

Michael and Marie could telepathically sense him and Chelo had continued to monitor his ocular implant in case it went live.

"Chelo, do you think you can hack the implant long enough for Michael to broadcast the feed to the world?"

"Yes, that's it!" Aissa was inspired.

A few minutes later as Michael looked down at Asante's closed eyes--so did millions of people watching television worldwide. He stepped back to reveal the faces of everyone seated in the circle around her and stopped at Aissa.

"I know the chains of fear have you bound, but I am speaking to the part of you that knows freedom even if you've never touched it. The part of you that knows something has never been quite right. The highest part of yourself because there you know the truth. We are here in New York City able to bring you this message because Asante, who now lays unconscious, gave herself completely to this moment. A moment that The Sephiren will do everything in their power to distract you from. The Now. Because in *The Now* they are killing us. Not just those of us condemned by the Declaration of War because we threaten their carefully constructed reality, but Americans from every walk of life, survivors of the travesty The Sephiren caused, are being brutalized outside of this very building. We have hacked into one of the ocular monitoring devices used by The Sephiren on one such American in the midst of this attack on the ground. In a moment we'll broadcast what he sees. Proof of our claims. After which I'll ask something of the part of you that knows the truth." Aissa stopped speaking for a moment and the feed cut to black for a few seconds.

Images of Brennan's ocular implant began to display on millions of monitors across the world. It was devastating to witness. A total massacre. The men in all black were killing without mercy. Men, women, and children were all being targeted without defense. The Wave members were making an impact, but they clearly couldn't keep up with the arsenal that the assassins used. They were being picked off one by one and being driven back toward the library.

The screen went black for another few seconds and Aissa appeared once more, this time tears poured down her face.

"This is what they think of you. This is what they think of us, not worthy of life if we don't submit to their control. The Sephiren sent these men here to kill us and will be inside this building in a few minutes. And the hope for humanity will be erased from the earth, a hope that our ancestors planted in the depths of our collective consciousness.

"We only have right now. We need you to believe, we need you to join us in making the impossible possible, *right now*. In the Bible, it says we can move mountains with just a mustard seed of faith. It is time to harvest that seed. This library is the mountain we need to move. This building is made up of the same molecules as everything else in this universe including ourselves. So don't think of it as something outside of yourself, think of moving this building as you would your arm. Now, I'm going to count backward from ten to one breathing deeply between each number. As I inhale, envision our protection covering the outside of this building in mirrors, as I exhale release any thought or fear that might block our intention. With the subsequent breaths, inhale our movement out of this location and exhale us to a place of peace, a place of protection, a place unseen by The Sephiren that we may have time to orchestrate our next move on your behalf."

Aissa began the countdown. As she did, Michael instructed Brennan to take cover and watch the library. Michael once again broadcasted from the ocular implant. At first, nothing seemed to be happening outside of the chaos that continued all around. Then the earth beneath the ground began to break apart around the perimeter of the library. With each collective breath and sound of

Aissa's words repeated by millions around the world, the building began to separate from the earth.

*   *   *

"Are you watching this?" Douglas and Fairchild burst into Farraday's office. Emily was watching the television with terror written across her face and fear in her heart. Her mind raced. She needed to stop this. Someone had disabled the kill switch in the device in Brennan's implant. The world was about to realize what they were really capable of.

"Finally," she whispered, "Find him and kill him now."

"Who? What are you talking about?" Douglas demanded.

"Brennan. He's on the ground. It's his feed that Michael is broadcasting!" She screamed.

"Send Brennan's picture to the assassins in their headsets, now, now," Fairchild yelled into his phone.

The building was about one hundred feet in the air when the surface began to change from stone and cement to a reflective substance as if it were made of mirrors. When it reached an altitude of nearly a thousand feet off of the ground it seemed to oscillate in the reflection of the sun. Then it disappeared altogether as Brennan looked into the sky with tears in his eyes. It was the most beautiful image he had seen in his whole life. It was also the last thing he saw before the bullet pierced the back of his head, killing him.

The television screen went black in Farraday's office.

"It's too late," was all Emily Farraday could say. Then her knees buckled beneath her, and she fell back into the seat behind her.

Chapter 25
Rosalyn

Something warm and wet was tickling Asante's toes. She noticed its touch was rhythmic, that it followed the pace of her slow breath. She opened her eyes. At first, she could not make out what she was looking at. It felt like the sky but the colors were hues of magenta, swirling with lavender and gold. She sat up to find herself sitting on a beach just as the tide met the sand. In front of her, the sun was on the horizon, but it was too large and bright to be real. It took up the majority if her peripheral view. It was too close.

Where am I? She thought. She looked down at her hands and her skin, though still olive-brown, it was translucent with a million little diamonds that sparkled like stars in the reflection of the sun. Yet the sight of her altered state didn't frighten her. Instead, a calm came over her and she knew true peace for the first time in her life. Am I dead?

The last thing she remembered was the silver-haired woman and Stella in the tsunami. She stood up and looked behind her. There were trees that looked like a dense jungle at the edge of the beach. Asante decided that she wasn't going in there, so she sat back down and decided to wait. She didn't know for what, but she also didn't know what else to do. As she looked directly into the sun the warmth of it embodied her and she closed her eyes. When she opened them a moment later the sun, though still on the horizon, seemed to be eclipsed by the moon. And the sky was now dark and filled with the stars that mirrored the diamonds under her skin. Asante began to cry not because she was scared, but because she was free.

As she wiped her eyes she could see something moving in the light of the moon. The movement took form and walked toward her out of the eclipsed sun; it was a woman. As she moved closer, Asante could see that she was dressed in a white and purple sheer gown that glowed like a thousand stars and bellowed in the wind. The water beneath her feet shone with a beautiful iridescent light. When the woman reached her, Asante lowered her head in reverence from the power emanating from this being. The woman then bent down and took Asante's hand in her own, which she noticed was made of the same olive-brown, translucent, and starry skin. Asante rose to look the woman in the eyes and realized it was her mother.

Stella embraced her daughter. A love without loss or pain of any kind entered, then engulfed every molecule of Asante's body. She became a part of the light as she leaned back to look at her mother's smiling face again. But as she did her mother's face changed into another woman that Asante didn't know but still was familiar, then another, and another, until a myriad of a hundred faces flashed in a moment, until the countenance of the woman holding her was that of the silver-haired woman from the tsunami. Asante reached out and held one of her long braids in her hand. Asante looked into her eyes deeply and exhaled her name, "Rosalyn."

The woman smiled and said, "Asante, the timeless."

Asante took in her familiar voice and said, "I know you, but how?"

"You've always known me and all of your ancestors. You have just been experiencing the constructs of the dimension you were in, as do all men when they take form."

Somehow this wasn't confusing for Asante and she accepted it with perfect understanding.

"So have I died, is that why I'm here with you now?" asked Asante.

"No my dear child, but you have begun to use the part of yourself that transcends the realm where your form exists. Thus, the universe must reflect this shift and has created this space from which the culmination of the formless and form can coexist in the same plane." Rosalyn explained.

"So this is not a dream, but a real place!"

Asante exclaimed looking around at all the beauty which surrounded them.

"Yes."

"So where is everyone?" Asante asked earnestly.

"In the world in which you left, it still exists, still trapped by form and time," said Rosalyn.

"So we are in a new age? But how if The Sephiren still has the world trapped in its guise? How can this place and that place exist at the same time, doesn't the old have to end for the new to begin?"

Rosalyn smiled at Asante and said, "No, those are concepts that only exist in time. The Sephiren is not the creator of the guise over man. It only facilitated it forward during the progression of form until this moment. Form needed time to evolve, to experience its self as such. The formless part of man has been dormant or largely hidden from his visage, but your life illustrates the reunification of form and formless as one."

"But The Sephiren, The Wave, and the rest of humanity doesn't understand that. They are still entrenched with time and are tied to the constructs The Sephiren have created that give meaning to their existence. And the members of The Wave are aiming to set man free from those constructs, not able to see their purpose."

"Well, that's why you were created. It's all a part of your covenant in entering into form, the shift has begun, you have experienced it there and have created it here, there is no difference in these realities other than in the minds and hearts of men. You will be the light that directs them to these shores." Rosalyn gave reassuringly.

"I still don't understand how? I still don't see clearly the choice I made that has had me arrive here?"

"Do you remember when you first opened the bridge so that the formless could take form? We had been leaving you hints through your attention with clues that point to the infinite, like repeating numbers on clocks or destinations."

"Yes! I had been waking at 5:55 for weeks just before my alarm was to go off." Asante whispered recalling the memory.

"And what did you allow yourself to be completely motivated by the morning of the surgery?"

Asante thought of Seager's family and his daughter's eyes that touched her so deeply.

"Love." She responded.

Rosalyn smiled immensely as it all began to click in Asante's understanding.

"So, The Now is the bridge and love is the vessel that brought the power of the formless into form." Asante surmised as the understanding flowed through her.

"Exactly my child. But know that you are the first, but you are not unique in this ability. Each person in form has the ability. It's how this place will expand into the new paradise for all to exist harmoniously."

"Now open your eyes and make it so," Rosalyn said warmly.

"But how do I get them to see?" Asante asked, still at a loss as to her next move.

"My child, that is a part of your covenant, I have no idea, but we will be ready as you need us, trust yourself and the rest will follow," Rosalyn said as she hugged Asante once more, then turned and walked back on top of the water into the setting eclipsed sun. Asante opened her eyes.

Chapter 26
A New Reality

Unbridled anarchy spread through the cities of the world in the following weeks after Aissa guided millions of people's energy to levitate and teleport The New York City Library. The knowledge that The Sephiren had been manipulating humankind in every aspect of life had taken root in the minds of millions. However, millions more refused to accept the foundational idea in which this reality was built upon. For many, the concept that they had not been in control of their own lives was too far of a stretch from the freedom they had been brainwashed to believe they already had. Those thirsty for the taste of real liberty and those comforted by their chains began to battle.

The first arena of combat was on the political stage. There was an immediate demand for new governance throughout the world. Political parties split into factions that no longer represented the ideologies that separated us for generations, yet a new division grew in its place. Those seeking The Now demanded an end to all that had previously defined and distracted humanity from its highest self. They wanted an end to nationalism, racism, sexism, and classism. A new world order with men, women, and children represented equally amongst those acting on their behalf.

The other side viewed these people as treasonous. Those still enslaved to the paradigm, rooted in time, couldn't let go of history, culture, and the traditions that were the foundation of their existence. They demanded the status quo be restored.

The second sphere of conflict rose for the spiritual identity of humankind. Many religious people that were trapped in their doctrine believed The Wave were cultists peddling dark magic disguised as enlightenment. Some Muslim, Christian, and Jewish leaders unified under this banner, calling Asante the Anti-Christ, which gratified the seeds of doubts in their followers' hearts which The Wave and Asante's abilities planted. Those that were never satisfied with traditional, false religious structures were open to thinking of their spiritual purpose in a new way. They began to organize under the ideas that The Wave pointed to, love and spiritual unification for all. The lines between these factions of belief became harder and more defined as neither The Wave nor The Sephiren voiced their allegiance to any side.

Many speculated on the whereabouts of where the library had been teleported. Some were convinced they were in another dimension. While others launched search parties in some of the most remote locations on the planet to no avail. Speculation also broke out about who were the members of The Sephiren. Some of the employees of Quanta came forward claiming that they had been on the ground level of the organization and that billionaire Eric Fairchild, media tycoons, The Vanderneiss', the late Dr. Louis Schmidt, Dr. Emily Farraday, and a long list of prominent politicians, scientists, and businessmen and women from all walks of life, all over the world, were all part of the unseen hand of The Sephiren. However, without proof, their voices were dissolved into the sea of emerging conspiracies on the matter.

When Aissa, Michael, and the others opened their eyes to the sound of The New York City Library settling into the earth they were all filled with a moment of relief. But when they stepped outside to find they were on a clearing next to Leigh Lake in Teton, Wyoming, an overwhelming sense of gratitude for life itself sprung from the depths of their souls. The beauty of the location reflected the millions of people's hope for a new reality. By all accounts, there were a hundred or so that survived the attack in New York and made it back inside the library before they all disappeared into the sky. For the next two days, they would contemplate their options while they healed.

With no communication with the rest of the world, they were at odds over their direction. Many members desired to stay off-grid while the repercussions of what happened unfolded. Michael felt they needed to organize and rebuild under the radar until The Sephiren's intentions could be revealed. But Aissa felt as though they should seize the moment and make their selves known capitalizing on what happened in New York. She was convinced that the world was awake and waiting for them.

"But what if you're wrong Aissa, are you willing to risk the destruction of The Wave on humanity's ability to free itself? We are on fragile ground here, we have less numbers now amongst us than any other time in history. The light that we are might completely go out with a move like this, I'm definitely not as confident in the hearts and minds of men anymore." J.StaRR stated in the middle of a heated debate on the subject.

"The point is, I am, and if there aren't any more objections, I'm open to suggestions on how we are going to go about taking that risk?"

"I have one," Asante said, startling them all as she sat up on the make-shift bed, where she had laid for the past few days.

Marie jumped up and screamed with surprise. Chelo and the others got up and rushed to Asante. They all had been distraught over the idea of her never waking up again, but had also started to hold firm to the idea that she would be the catalyst behind their forward motion if she had died, regardless of the direction. At this moment, all of that was replaced with overflowing joy. Aissa, Michael, and Chelo kissed and hugged her first.

After greeting everyone present Asante said, "I need some water and time. I have so much to tell you, but I don't know how yet."

They all looked at each other in confusion as Marie gave Asante water. Asante then cleared her throat after drinking and begged, "Please, I need to be alone."

Though no one wanted to leave her, Michael nodded first, and put his hands on Chelo and Aissa's shoulders and began to guide them toward the exit of the large hall where they had set up camp around Asante. Everyone present followed suit.

She first called Michael back in to speak with her a few hours later. She had used the time to try and figure out the best explanation of what she had experienced with Stella and Rosalyn. But her words fell short.

"I know what we must do, but first I need you to understand the place from which I now view the world and my place in its story. The best way to do that is for you to read my mind in search of the memories of where I was while I lay unconscious here."

Not truly understanding what Asante meant, but eager to find out, Michael stepped forward, placed his two fingers on each of her temples and closed his eyes. A few moments later he opened his eyes with tears streaming down his face.

"What's wrong, Daddy?" Asante asked compassionately.

"The sight of your mother's face and the truth which you must bear fills my heart with joy and sadness."

Asante drew closer to understand him better.

"I'm so pleased that this is your journey. I'm amazed at how close I was to understanding but yet so far away from seeing the whole truth.

"As I've told you in the past, love is your greatest weapon, but almost losing you is still fresh in my mind and I can't help but fear for your life."

Asante stroked his hand then looked into her Daddy's eyes and said, "We are all but vessels tasked with bringing the formless into form, I am the accumulation of form progressing over time, but I am not the only one. We all will create this paradise we were intended for, whether I am in this form should no longer bring you pain, but if it does now, there will be a point when it doesn't, let that give you hope while you journey."

Michael stared at her in awe, she was no longer growing into The Aurora but was fully embodying the very notion it pointed to. We are all one.

Though Asante could feel Aissa's apprehensions, she decided that this was not the time to dissolve them. She instead greeted Aissa with gentle compassion.

"Did you miss me?" Asante smiled broadly into her question.

"More than I thought possible, I thought I lost you." The words barely escaped her mouth before she was almost hysterical with emotion. She collapsed into Asante's arms.

For a few long moments, they were just two little girls lost in their love for one another.

"Asante The Aurora, how do you feel?"

"Like I'm going to need you more than ever, the world is ready to move forward, are you?"

"I'm ready to destroy The Sephiren, the world is ready to be set free!" Aissa's voice was wild with passion.

"Your enthusiasm will be needed on the front lines of our movement, trust it and keep it close to your heart."

Although Asante's words weren't in opposition to Aissa's feelings, she could feel the new depth from which her sister spoke and knew Asante had found authority in being The Aurora. Aissa was filled with pride, yet dissatisfaction with her own role brimmed beneath the surface.

After everyone reconvened and met individually with Asante, the new direction was clear, they would re-enter society in the United States. Asante would stay in Teton, Wyoming teaching the new aims of The Wave while convoys would go back on grid, gathering supplies and technology, so that they wouldn't be walking into an ambush or create more chaos in the emerging new world. They spent the next three months making the damaged library their new edifice of learning while silent to the outside world.

Finally, at the dawn of spring, they sent a message to The Sephiren to the attention of Dr. Emily Farraday for a meeting on the dark web. Within moments she responded. To everyone's dismay and protest, Asante requested their meeting be in Teton, Wyoming at their new headquarters. She wouldn't risk any more casualties. Though no one was confident in the plan, their hope lied within the heart of Asante. They would follow her anywhere.

When a single black Tesla Model X was spotted driving fifty miles west of Leigh Lake; final preparations began in their new headquarters. Nothing could be detected from the Satellite or Wave operated drones other than a single driver in the Model X. Asante led a meditation in the final moments before Farraday's arrival for healing, understanding, peace, and ultimately cooperation.

Emily Farraday had been wallowing in a mix of self-pity and rage since New York. She couldn't process what had occurred because it went against her very deep sense that she was the victor. She had been querying Quantum incessantly and by all accounts, this time of unrest would pass and The Sephiren would take root again in the hearts and minds of the people. However, that's not what the world looked like, even though the majority were still cloaked in distraction, more and more people were waking up every day, creating more doubt in the minds of the masses. It reminded Emily of an infectious disease, which inspired her new phase for The Sephiren. Create the ultimate mechanism in which total control would no longer be a complicit act the masses participated in, but a voluntary one. It was while exploring this mechanism, that Emily received Asante's message.

"Perfect timing dear niece," Farraday quickly responded to the request to meet.

As she pulled up to the coordinates that the message had indicated for the meeting, Michael and Obadias stood in the dusk of the night's cold air as her headlights flashed over their bodies. Their breath could be seen coming out of their scarfed necks. Farraday's dashboard read nineteen degrees. She grabbed her fur and exited the vehicle.

"Nice to see you, Michael," She said coolly.

"We go on foot from here." He stated in response as he and Obadias turned and began to walk into the forest.

"How far is it?" Farraday asked.

"Does it matter?" Michael retorted.

The rest of the five-mile hike was spent in silence.

The library had been converted similarly to the layout of the Mayacamas Headquarters on a larger scale but still had much work to be done before it would be a secure structure. Though it was after eight pm by the time Emily, Michael, and Obadias arrived, the place was still busy with people working to establish the security of the infrastructure. Everyone had a job and after the meditation moments before, Asante had instructed that they get to it while she met with Emily alone.

Asante was in a state of purpose, clarity, and peace when Emily entered the room of reflection. Asante sat looking out onto the mist rolling over Leigh Lake illuminated by the external lights of the building. As Emily took her first step into the room she could feel the energy emanating from Asante, this was not the same girl from the Gateway Facility. The woman who now sat before her was just as confident as Emily. Finally, a worthy adversary she thought.

"What do you want?" Farraday jumped in.

Asante was ready, "Ironically the same as you."

"Don't be cute, you know as well as I do that our interests are diametrically opposed," Farraday replied, losing some of her cool.

"Only if you choose to look at it that way, but I know we both want what's in the best interest for humanity. We only differ on our perspective of what that is, but I have come to see it as a necessary step in the evolution of human beings.

"We can't change what's happened, what we've been a part of creating up until this point. But we can stand together in this new reality that is unfolding and give humankind something they've never had access to previously." Answered Asante. She waited as her words settled in the heart and mind of her aunt.

"And what might that be?" Farraday asked cautiously.

"A conscious informed choice," Asante replied. Emily's eyes grew wide and the currents of blue electricity could be seen in her pupils. This had been her aim all along. But before she gave her definitive response, she asked one more question.

"Define conscious?"

"We come forward and imbue these factions that have sprung forth from our war with knowledge, then they can decide. From their decision, not ours, will a new direction for humanity come forth and we agree right here and now to not interfere with the opposing ideology. We focus only on illuminating what we believe and a safe space for those in agreement to exist." Asante smiled.

"What are you really suggesting?" Farraday asked as the implication of Asante's plan began to enter her own consciousness.

Asante walked to an armoire in the corner of the room, opened it up and pulled out a map of the world and laid it on the floor in front of them, "I'll show you what I mean, let's get started."

Chapter 27
The Choice

The years following Asante and Emily's meeting by the lake in the heartland of America were of exploration and transition. The new frontier that they chose that night would transform the face of not only the United States but of every nation in the world. Each woman started on a path that evening that they would journey until the end of time. They took their first steps a few weeks later when Emily Farraday gathered all the leaders of The Sephiren in a televised news conference at the Palace of Westminster in London. Besides The Sephiren's leaders, in attendance were representatives of political and religious groups from around the globe.

"We have gathered here today to present the world with a choice. A choice based on the foundation of what it means to be human." Emily Farraday began as she stood in the hall where three hundred years previous the voices of men were heard and paved the road to the fork where the world now stood.

"The Sephiren has been making this choice for mankind since the dawn of civilization." Gasps of shock coupled with disbelief could be heard throughout the chamber. "And in that time we've been responsible for the progression of humanity. Just think where the world was only three hundred years ago when this building housed the first parliament of Great Britain. Humanity has had its shining moments as well as its darkest hours, but all-in-all we've been a part of man successfully continuing to move through time." She paused while applause sprinkled throughout the hall.

"So the choice that we have been burdened to carry for you has been for all of our benefit. We only have had all of our best interests in mind, which was the intention of our founders when The Sephiren was created. So what I'm about to say may sound jarring at first, but if you give me a moment to explain all will become clear." She paused again to wait for her words to sink into the minds of all that watched her from around the world.

"Just as we have provided order for the steps of men, The Wave has been attempting to provide a viable alternative as well. One which our founders, as well as ourselves, believe will bring an end to all that we have accomplished.

"But here we are, and just as humanity has evolved, so must we. The Sephiren will no longer be an unseen hand working on behalf of you, but a partner, collaboratively working with you." Applause sprinkled through the hall.

"The Wave believes, if given a choice, man will not continue down the path that has been our destiny since the dawn of time, but travel to a new place where our history and the backbone of our achievements don't exist. So the choice we are asking you to make is not one of nation, creed, or religion but of consciousness. Continue with us through time together at the helm of your definition amongst the infinite. Continue to enjoy life as you know it or dissolve into the abyss of the unknown and possibility that The Wave offers." Applause now erupted in the hall and in the hearts of hundreds of millions of people around the world.

"In light of this choice we know that education and restructure must happen first. So we have met with The Wave and have agreed to each hold a conference to facilitate moving forward in transparency and peace. The destruction of the eastern seaboard of the United States, as well as the millions of lives lost, is an error that neither side would like to repeat.

"Today is the first day of our summit and it will run for the next hundred days. In that time the new map of the world will begin to form. In the Northern Hemisphere, the way of The Sephiren will be reestablished, only now with new governance and elections based upon our unified choice to continue down the halls of time. In the Southern Hemisphere of the world, The Wave will establish the same based upon their aims. I now will open the floor to questions for the next hour, then we will need to begin the process of defining our next steps."

*   *   *

"That went better than expected," Chelo asserted to Asante as he turned off the television monitor.

He started to massage her back ten minutes before The Wave would broadcast their message and subsequent conference. Asante and Emily had purposefully timed their announcements and reintroduction to the world a few minutes apart in order to give their messages an opportunity to fairly resonate in the hearts and minds of humankind.

The leaders of The Wave had all arrived in Johannesburg, South Africa the morning before. Marie and J.StaRR had scouted the perfect location for Asante to speak to the masses, The Creative Counsel building. Not only had representatives from most nations come to meet with her, but religious leaders, scientists, engineers, and provocative artists from every medium came to cast their say in the emerging new landscape. While at their summit, the Zen garden on the property would serve as the backdrop to cement the foundation of the new choice The Wave would offer. Although Asante immensely enjoyed the massage that Chelo was administering, she wasn't tense at all and she felt he may be working out his own misgivings.

"What's wrong?" They asked simultaneously, they smiled at one another as Chelo turned Asante around to face him.

Asante could sense what he was feeling, but waited for the thought to form in his own mind so that he could articulate it. She never knew him to be as vulnerable as he was in this moment.

"I've always known your greatness, it's given me hope and courage to be who I am, not only for myself but for you, but in a few moments the world will know it, and for the first time I am fearful if we can exist in this new world you're creating, if who I am will matter in this new paradigm?" Chelo said as he put his head down almost ashamed of his fear.

Asante lifted his chin so that their eyes could meet, "The first seeds of who I am, were firmly planted in my heart and mind by your love, it was a reminder of what I had forgotten, distracted by time. But as you showed me, when we first met, we've always been and will always be, our love wasn't created in time but is as formless and infinite as the universe itself." With this, they embraced, kissed deeply and walked to the Zen garden to meet the world.

"My name is Dr. Asante Argueta," Asante said into the microphone at the podium located at the back of the garden. "I include my credentials here in my introduction for two very important reasons. First, because contrary to what you've been told, my aim is to not erase what we've brought into form or creation because that is a part of who we are, a part of our purpose. But the second reason I mention my credentials is that I want you to know that how you have chosen to define yourself directs your attention to who you are amongst the infinite. In my case, I am a vessel for healing, of restoration. But I only came into the full view of what that meant after I let go of all the distractions of life. Distractions rooted in time perpetuated and reinforced by The Sephiren. So I am, we are, offering a choice. A choice to live and experience life without these distractions, so that the highest potential of form can create a paradise where the infinite can be experienced without fear. We are connected to the world around us, not only by what we can touch physically, but we are connected in the formless part of everything that exists.

"The best way to describe it is that we are all connected through frequency, so we can transform the world around us by connecting to it harmoniously through a wave of sorts. We want to teach you how to access and ride those waves, but first, we must connect to The Wave within. The only way to do that is through The Now. For the first time in history, we want to shift our focus from what happened and what will happen to what is happening. Yes, it's unknown territory, but it is one we can explore together!"

Everyone in the garden stood in a roar of applause and cheering. Millions around the world stood ready to walk into the abyss of the unknown with Asante.

After the respective one hundred day summits, the great transition began, marked by mass migrations all over the world. A border was set up at the equator and Wave or Sephiren documentation replaced traditional citizenship papers redefining identity.

Although families, business conglomerates, and financial institutions were torn apart, the spirit of cooperation and desire for peace in this new world prevailed at first. The number of people under the leadership of The Sephiren still outnumbered The Wave seven to one. After a year of mass relocation, a billion people lived in the new reality of The Wave. But over the next two years, while education and training in the principles of The Wave became firmly planted in the people that number would grow to three billion.

Fear on both sides began to erupt. Emily and the other members of the Council felt that their dwindling numbers would prove to be a fatal blow to the greatest level of control The Sephiren had ever known. While for Asante and The Wave the reality of space and resources were becoming a challenge for each new soul seeking freedom in The Wave.

Both sides agreed to enter into a pact for a generation where they levied the amount of resources from The Sephiren with a waitlist of people seeking to cross the border. The New Transition Treaty of 2020 was the best compromise for both sides. But despite the intentions of the treaty, the spirit of cooperation dissolved into unrest and corruption and the choice disappeared.

Chapter 28
T.O.R.N.

The Sephiren's territory-wide mandate for ocular implants was the first of many alterations to the fabric of the new deception called transparency that was implemented by Emily Farraday shortly after the borders closed. A new society emerged where human point of view became a commodity.

One's ability to lead the most entertaining and extravagant life, while being broadcast into the homes of the marginally mundane became the pinnacle achievement in this society. Real estate in the areas in which these people led their lives skyrocketed. New luxurious metropolises were established. While the areas where the majority of the population lived became large slum cities that were a breeding ground for a spirit of rebellion.

In a city that used to be New Orleans a hacker soon acquired the ability to interrupt his feed and go offline while streaming recorded feed for periods of time undetected. He eventually set up a system, first with his girlfriend Neda, where they'd exchange information offline. However, to do so, an intricate timing schedule was developed where they were never offline at the same time. Code was created to leave clues in plain sight while their feeds were live but unnoticeable to the average Sephiren Observer who was tasked with weeding out rebellion. The SO were the new law enforcement in the territory and there was a task force within it dedicated to building cases against individuals based on information gathered through their feeds.

This kept the masses in line with The Sephiren's agenda like never before. But this hacker used clues that would create a code that pinpointed rendezvous location and instructions to further their cause. In a few years' time, their numbers grew to a few thousand. In that time the hacker was able to create a mini quantum computer. This facilitated their numbers to exponentially grow to a few million. The only thing this hacker couldn't figure out was how to contact Asante and The Wave and convince her to overthrow Farraday and The Sephiren. He was dreaming of this when his alarm rang and the clock displayed 4:44 am for the third day in a row, though he had set it to 5:00 am.

"Again!" Neda yelled, pushing her pillow into his face.

While his eyes were still closed, in the darkness behind his lids the word *Teton* appeared in white block letters.

"Teton," he said out loud.

"What'd you call me, Elijah Remy Farraday!" Neda asked.

"Nothing." He said as he made a mental note. He knew Emily Farraday had been watching him since before the reformation of the world. His uncle and guardian Ezra had been preparing him his whole life for this moment, which is why he chose to stay in Sephiren Territory, he knew he'd have to take Emily Farraday down from within.

Over the next twenty-four hours, he would create code for Neda to find in order for her to start research on the word Teton. Within a week they had discovered that an old Wave Headquarters in The New York City Library was still standing at Leigh Lake in Teton, Wyoming. He couldn't risk going there himself, so within a month, a team was formed and a reconnaisance mission planned amongst the rebellion. He had a feeling that some clue was left there for him in Teton to find. He decoded a message that a download with information from the mission awaited for him off-feed. After disrupting his ocular implant, he set a timer for twenty minutes and streamed his recorded feed. He then pressed a button on his keychain that also doubled as a remote to access a secret room in his and Neda's Parisian loft. He sat at the console for his mini quantum computer and downloaded the file.

After a few moments of analyzing the data streaming across his monitor, he realized what he was looking at, a backdoor. It was a backdoor to access The Sephiren's Quantum computer completely undetectable. Within moments he was in. Inside Farraday's personal files, he found a folder named "2050 D-Day". But he couldn't access it. He didn't have much time. He found one more door entitled, "T.O.R.N.", just as he was about to encrypt the backdoor from which he entered Quantum. Before he exited the secret chamber he left himself some notes and one message for Neda. *What is TORN?*

*   *   *

Aissa had been given the responsibility of Deputy Director of the South American Territory of The Wave and subsequent border protection. Although she missed Asante, running her own territory where she was able to oversee the curriculum for the education Asante wanted to be instructed in every land of The Wave territory gave her a sense of purpose and satisfied her need to lead.

Aissa established universities all over the territory where areas of study included courses on integration and entrainment, finding which frequency resonates within, and experiments in mass meditation. There were Art and Science centers in every province of the territory where interactive exhibits took the visitors through experiences that the mediums had never achieved before. Telepathic experiments were done to send messages throughout the territory that became the beginning of new security measures for The Wave. It was a new age in a dawn of redefining humanity.

Every morning Aissa and Obadias would surf the coastline of Mancora, Peru, where they lived. They were close enough to the border that if anything came up, she could be there within hours, but still were able to wake up in a literal paradise as the backdrop of creating this new world. However, Aissa couldn't help but feel dissent when Asante agreed to close the borders. She understood it from a place of self-preservation and limited resources, Asante didn't want to establish trade with The Sephiren, not if it could be avoided. But the compassion for those still enslaved but hoping for freedom out of the terror that had become the reality of living under the transparency laws of The Sephiren's Regime was nonexistent under the new treaty. Aissa heard stories that broke her heart—of torture and executions of those suspected of rebellion, broadcast territory-wide. She had made up her mind that regardless of Asante's directives to keep the treaty, she could not let the innocent continue to die.

"If only we knew how many people wanted out of The Sephiren Territory and could organize them—that might change her mind," Aissa said to Obadias while they walked back from surfing to their beachfront property in Mancora.

"We've been through this, the new grid with Quantum as its mechanism and the ocular implants as its data point for each person in the territory is impossible to permeate. In the treaty, Michael and Obadias are specifically outlined—as well as any other person with the ability to interfere with their system—as deal-breakers if found to be meddling in the affairs of The Sephiren and their territories.

"There's peace on earth, we chose to live in this reality and they chose as well, when the treaty period is up, I'm sure we will have found a solution to the resource problem and Asante will reassess the terms of the treaty." Obadias repeated to her his position as he had done many times before.

"But that's nearly thirty years from now. What if their hope is eradicated by then?" But to this Obadias just shook his head; he had no answer for her.

*   *   *

After many months of precisely timed espionage, Elijah finally figured out what the other door in The Sephiren's Quantum computer mainframe was designed to do. It was a portal of sorts, but it could only send out one two-hundred-eighty character message. But there was no way of telling who would receive the message. Although he had reservations that this might all be a trap by Emily Farraday to finish what she set out to do many moons prior, he hoped that his message would get to Asante. More importantly, he hoped that he had the words to touch her heart. He spent every moment he was off-feed trying to construct the message, but nothing accurately depicted what he was after. He decided to speak from his own heart. It was all they had left.

I am Elijah Farraday. I am assisting those left behind journey to freedom. I risked everything to send this message, millions seeking hope rest in the fate of my words, so I leave you with what you left me, the fate of your world and mine depend upon it, There's Only Right Now.

Epilogue
Farrah & Soraya

The touch of eyelashes against her cheek was the first thing Asante felt as she slowly opened her eyes. Little high pitched giggles followed. She quickly shut her lids and laid as still as possible. Next, a small elbow pushed down into her chest and a knee felt like it was trying to escape through her back via her abdomen. She took a breath as she stilled her body, then before they could escape, she grabbed both of her girls and wrestled them underneath her so she could begin her form of revenge.

"You dare to wake the sleeping tickle monster, you will pay, you will pay now!" Asante yelled at the top of her lungs as she tickled Farrah and Soraya. Born a few moments apart nothing could separate the two. Sometimes they were able to trick her and Chelo as to their identities. Besides being the most identical set of twins that Asante had ever seen, they were so very much alike in energy, preferences, and personality. When they were born, they hugged each other in their crib constantly, if pulled apart for any reason, even to feed, they'd cry and wine until they were reunited. They spent every waking moment together of their four years alive.

All of the commotion on her side of the bed still didn't wake a sleeping Chelo who was buried under a pile of pillows and blankets.

After Asante's love attack on their little bodies, she put her finger over her mouth and whispered, "Let's get Daddy."

The girls loved this part of their morning ritual best. They snuck under the blankets and began to move toward Chelo's body like little moles moving through the ground.

Just as they reached his body for their own tickle attack, Asante pulled back the covers and yelled "Wonder Twins, go! Attack, attack!"

As the girls began to tickle their father with all their might, he swooped them up in his arms and began to kiss them all over.

"This never gets old, best way to wake up!" Chelo said as he smiled and looked into Asante's eyes.

"Who wants strawberry jacks?" Asante asked her family.

Soraya, Chelo, and Farrah raised their hands simultaneously as if they wanted to be called on first in class and shouted, "Me!" in unison.

Asante grabbed her robe and said *lights* as she entered the hallway outside her door. Little LED lights illuminated the ground as she took each step. She preferred this setting this early in the morning as the sky was still dark with hues of violet and purple rising from the horizon in the distance. She took the glass staircase to the second floor of their three-story apartment in Johannesburg's tallest sky rise. The second floor had a three-sixty view of the city because of its floor to ceiling windows that encompassed the living space. In the center of the space, an open all-white and copper kitchen greeted her. She was still amazed that she was able to keep it pristine every time she entered it. She made herself a matcha latte and began to make her favorite strawberry jacks.

Asante filled the last of the cups with freshly squeezed orange juice from the refrigerator dispenser and brought them to the table where her family sat. Soraya reached for a piece of pancake.

Asante said, "You know we give thanks first." They all took three clearing breaths, and Asante began, "In gratitude and love we enter in this moment, we nurture our form as we allow the formless to flow through. Ashe."

"Ashe," They all repeated. As the word left her lips, the blowing in Asante's ears began. She hadn't felt it since she met Rosalyn. The hairs on her arms stood up.

"What's wrong?" Chelo asked.

"I'm not sure."

She got up from the table and walked to one of the windows. Nothing. Clear.

She waited.

The blowing became a rushing wind in her ears. Still nothing. She turned back to walk toward the table where her family waited for her. She smiled at them, taking in each one of their beautiful faces. Chelo still took her breath away with his piercing eyes. Soraya and Farrah both had tight, dark-brown, curly hair whose ringlets were sun-kissed with auburn. Their caramel-olive skin framed their huge light brown eyes as if drawn to perfection. Five steps before she reached the table all the windows that encompassed the apartment shattered at once, shards of glass shot in every direction.

Asante threw up her arms creating a force field that shielded her and her family from the shards. A moment later she released the force field, the gushing wind that rushed through the apartment sent her tumbling into the table where she was able to grab Soraya just as she was being lifted out of her chair by the force of the wind. Chelo caught Farrah in the same manner.

Head toward the staircase, She heard Chelo's voice in her head.

Each step took every bit of her energy to accomplish. She reached into herself and pulled from the depths of her soul as she held her daughter as tight as she could. But it was as if the wind had a purpose, an intent, almost to separate her from her child. As she looked up, she could see that Chelo seemed to be having the same struggle, she heard him say in her head once more, *I'm losing her*, as the wind seemed to pry Farrah from his grasp.

Asante's heart dropped as she watched her baby fly from his hands into the wind and out of the apartment. Soraya looked up at her with fear and sadness. Asante had to hold on, she must, but the more she did the more aggressive the wind became. Chelo began to make his way through the force of the rushing wind toward them. *Just a little longer*, Asante thought. Then what seemed like an invisible hand of air snatched her remaining child from her hands. Soraya's screams rang in her head as the wind immediately stopped once her baby disappeared. Chelo was at her side as she moaned "NOOOOOOOOOO!"

*　　*　　*

The sound of her heels clicking against the marble floor as she approached her office always filled Emily Farraday with delight, but this morning she was especially pleased with herself. She took a moment and paused before she opened the door. Though they still weren't certain of the number of people associated with the rebellion, she could feel her control over the society she had meticulously created with such patience and discipline slipping from her grasp. She wasn't sure how but she knew Quantum had been compromised, she had been betrayed and at the heart of the betrayal was Asante.

But today all that would end. Today Asante would know the pain that only true loss provided, a feeling that Emily had known most of her life, a feeling she'd make sure Asante would know intimately for the rest of hers. She reveled in this thought a moment longer, then she finally opened the double doors, and looked around. Everything was in its place. Her steel desk and matching furniture gleamed in the mid-morning light.

"I know you're in here, where are you hiding?" She looked under the desk, nothing, opened her wardrobe closet, nothing. She then walked to the large potted Fern plant in the corner and pushed the leaves aside. "There you are!"

Crouched in the corner and hugging each other tightly with fear and tears in their eyes were two little girls. "I understand your names are Farrah and Soraya." They nodded their heads yes cautiously. "Nice to meet you," She held out her hands for the girls to shake them. "You can call me, Auntie Em."

About the Author

Ampora Yazdani learned at a young age that family is precious, storytelling is a gift, and hard work is everything. With pure will to drive her career, she worked her way up from intern to executive in the music business working for industry giants such as Bad Boy, J Records, Interscope, and Sony. During this time, she voraciously learned about the managing of the creative process while operating a business and nurturing relationships.

Building from this experience, she moved to Los Angeles to focus on developing her own creative work as she continued to consult for Sony while also partnering with her husband to grow the family business. She currently resides in Los Angeles with her husband and three kids.

To learn more about Ampora visit www.yazdaniworks.com or follow her on Instagram and Twitter @yazdanimami

Made in the USA
Las Vegas, NV
09 September 2022